ROBERT BLOCH was born in Chicago
in 1917 and was encouraged to write
by none other than the late H. P.
Lovecraft. He sold his first story at the
age of 17 and since that time has written
over 400 short stories, published 38
books, 14 of which are novels. His
British films include THE SKULL and
the scripts of PSYCHOPATH, THE
DEADLY BEES, TORTURE
GARDEN, THE HOUSE THAT
DRIPPED BLOOD and ASYLUM. He
won the coveted 'Hugo' award for the
best sf story in 1958, has twice been guest
of honour at World Science Fiction
Conventions. In 1970–1971 he was
President of the Mystery Writers of
America. He has also written scripts for
THRILLER, STAR TREK, NIGHT
GALLERY and ALFRED
HITCHCOCK PRESENTS (all of
which have been seen on British
television). He now lives in Los Angeles.
His best known work is, of course,
PSYCHO.

Also by Robert Bloch

PSYCHO
FIREBUG
THE SKULL OF THE MARQUIS DE SADE
NIGHT-WORLD

and published by Corgi Books

Robert Bloch

Atoms and Evil

CORGI BOOKS
A DIVISION OF TRANSWORLD PUBLISHERS LTD

ATOMS AND EVIL

A CORGI BOOK 0 552 10486 8

Originally published in Great Britain by Robert Hale Ltd.

PRINTING HISTORY
Robert Hale edition published 1976
Corgi edition published 1977

This book is set in Intertype Plantin

Corgi Books are published by
Transworld Publishers Ltd.,
Century House, 61–63 Uxbridge Road,
Ealing, London W5 5SA
Made and printed in Great Britain by
Cox & Wyman Ltd., London, Reading and Fakenham

CONTENTS

TRY THIS FOR PSIS

ONCE upon a time there was a sane scientist who had an ugly daughter.

The scientist's name was Dr. Angus Welk, and in the Anthropology Department of a large eastern university he was the brachycephalic head. He was, naturally, a staunch believer in the physical sciences. At the same time, he detested anything abstract. He had a particular hatred for that branch of scientific investigation known as parapsychology – the investigation of extrasensory perception and psychokinesis. 'There is absolutely no such thing as telepathy,' he often declared. 'It's all in your mind.'

Nor was Dr. Welk content to let the matter rest there. He made a constant habit of challenging every investigator in the field of ESP or psi phenomena. He heckled them at lectures, he wrote indignant letters to psychiatric journals, he published a long monograph entitled 'Extrasensory Deception'. And during his summer vacation, when his colleagues roamed over the New England states with their cameras, happily exposing film, Dr. Welk covered the same territory, happily exposing spiritualist mediums. So perhaps Dr. Welk was not completely sane.

And maybe his daughter, Nora, was not entirely ugly. True, everything about her was just a little larger than life-size. Her nose was a trifle big and her mouth was too wide, and her cheekbones were so prominent they might easily have run for public office. But in an era which bows down before the busts of Monroe, Loren, Lollobrigida and Ekberg, she possessed certain other attributes which might be considered outstanding. In fact, one might easily search the wide world over without finding her equal in either hemisphere.

It was not necessary, however, to conduct a global mission in order to discover Nora Welk's whereabouts. As a graduate student she served as her father's secretary, and also ran his household. Dr. Welk was a widower, and secretly considered himself fortunate in that his daughter had never shown the slightest interest in young men.

'When the right mate for you comes along,' he often told her, 'I'll let you know. I'll recognize him by his cephalic index, and we'll conduct a controlled experiment. A true eugenic mating, my dear. Won't that be nice?'

Nora used to agree that it would be just splendid, but as time went on she began to entertain doubts. Maybe that's because doubts were all she ever had to entertain – nobody asked her for a date, and whenever she timidly mentioned a young man's name in her father's presence he would denounce the individual as a dolichocephalic dolt.

Just how long they might have continued their sane, ugly life together is problematical – if a problem hadn't arisen in the shape of Frank Tallent.

Frank Tallent didn't have much of a shape. He was short, sandy-haired, and myopic, and weighed about a hundred and ten pounds, dripping wet – if he climbed on the bathroom scale with a heavy bar of soap in each hand.

But he happened to sit next to Nora Welk at a lecture one evening, and the damage was done.

All during the talk he kept staring at her profile, occasionally lifting his eyes to her face, and when the session ended he noticed that she seemed to have some trouble finding her purse.

As she groped about her, he touched her arm. 'I beg your pardon, Miss,' he said, 'but the purse is under your seat.'

Nora blinked at him. 'I just looked there,' she declared.

Frank Tallent reddened. 'I wasn't referring to the *wooden one*,' he murmured. 'If you'll just get up—'

Sure enough, there was the purse.

Now it was Nora's turn to blush. 'Thank you,' she said. 'I can't imagine how it got there. I guess I was so interested in the speech I didn't notice when it slid behind me.' She smiled at Frank. 'It *was* an interesting speech, wasn't it?'

'I thought it stunk,' Frank said, with more vehemence than grammar.

Nora's eyes flashed. 'Is that so? And just what was wrong with it, might I ask?'

'Why, that old goat doesn't know what he's talking about,' Frank answered. 'Just because you can't weigh it or measure it or put it under a microscope, he claims there isn't any such thing as clairvoyance.'

'I suppose you know differently?'

'Of course I do.' Frank peered up at her through his glasses. 'I'm taking a special course in the Psych Department, under Professor Seine. He's probably the most famous authority on parapsychology in the country.'

Nora sniffed. 'Professor Seine is a crackpot,' she declared. 'And the old goat who delivered tonight's lecture happens to be my father.'

She started to brush past Frank, but the young man reached out his hand and grabbed her by the elbow.

'Better empty out your purse first, before you go,' he said. 'The stopper came out of your perfume bottle and your things are getting soaked.'

Nora halted and scrabbled in her handbag.

'You're right!' she exclaimed. 'How on earth did you know?'

'I'm a psychic sensitive.' Frank answered, modestly. 'Dr. Seine is using me to run experiments. I could see what was going on inside your handbag. It isn't a matter of actual eyesight, you know.'

Nora started to nod, then shook her head. 'Of course not,' she agreed. 'It isn't eyesight at all. You could smell that perfume leaking and you just jumped to conclusions. My father says that's how Professor Seine distorts all his data. He's explained everything to me – but of course, *you* wouldn't be interested.'

'On the contrary, I'm very much interested,' Frank protested. 'Maybe you'd be good enough to tell me about your father's theories. Over a cup of coffee, perhaps?'

Nora hesitated a moment.

'I'll buy you a hamburger, too,' Frank went on. 'After all, you didn't eat any supper.'

'How did you know that?'

'Psychic.' Frank grinned faintly as he rose. Nora hesitated once more.

'Don't worry about your father,' Frank went on. 'He's backstage talking to the reporters, telling them what a fool Professor Seine is and what a courageous investigator *he* is.'

'Is that supposed to be another demonstration of your psyclear powers?' Nora inquired.

'Just a guess,' Frank admitted. 'But I'm right, aren't I?'

'Probably. Only you're wrong about my father and his theories. Let me tell you—'

So she told him over a hamburger, and over a cup of coffee, and over two cigarettes.

At the end of it all, Frank Tallent sighed. 'I'm sorry,' he said. 'I've heard all these arguments before. Table-tipping and levitation isn't telekinesis, but a fake. Mind-precognition in dreams is just coincidence, and so forth. But the trouble is, *I* can do these things. I do them every day, with Professor Seine. He says I'm the most remarkable subject he's seen since Lady, the Talking Horse.'

'Does he hypnotize you?' Nora asked, as they left the restaurant and walked along the darkened streets.

'Of course not. It's just something that seems to come naturally. I never knew I had ESP or psi powers at all until I came to the university and got into his class. He asked for volunteers one day when he was demonstrating telekinesis with a pair of dice, and I got up and threw thirty passes in a row. After that he took an interest in me.'

'Who wouldn't?' Nora scoffed. 'If I could throw thirty passes in a row I'd go to Las Vegas and make a fortune.'

'It isn't that easy,' Frank explained. 'Apparently the sub-liminal mind is influenced adversely by the conscious mind when the element of personal gain enters into the situation. I had the same idea after throwing the passes, of course. I got into a little crap game with some of the boys in my dormitory.'

'What happened?'

'I lost eighteen bucks the first five minutes.'

'You see?' Nora nodded. 'It doesn't really work. That's why none of these so-called mind readers ever make a killing on the stock market.'

'I explained about that,' Frank answered. 'You can't control the phenomena. And if you're seeking some kind of reward, you freeze up. But the fact remains, I *did* throw thirty straight passes with those dice in the classroom.'

'Then either the dice were loaded, or you were.'

'Impossible. Professor Seine is an honest man, and I don't drink.' Frank took the girl's arm as they entered the park and halted near a bench. 'If I could only make you understand,' he said. 'Sit down here a moment. Maybe I can give you a demon-stration.'

They took their places on the bench.

'Now,' Frank began. 'Take your feet off the ground. That's it. I'll do the same. We're sitting quietly, right? And the bench is firmly balanced on the grass, isn't it?'

'Yes.'

'Watch this,' Frank said.

Suddenly the bench beneath them began to move. It tipped forward and the girl, with a gasp of astonishment, slid into his arms.

'What happened?' she murmured.

'Telekinesis,' he told her, tightening his embrace. 'What do you think of it?'

'It's wonderful,' Nora sighed snuggling closer.

'Would you like another demonstration? How about a little supernormal perception?'

'Whatever you say.' Nora was beginning to feel quite conscious of this young man's psychic aura; it positively made her tingle all over. She had never dreamed that a scientific experiment could be so interesting.

To her disappointment, Frank released her suddenly and stood up.

'All right,' he said. 'Here's what you do. I'm going to walk over there and stand under that tree, with my back to you. I want you to take something out of your purse and hide it while I'm not looking. Then it's up to me to find it.'

Strictly in the spirit of scientific inquiry, Nora selected an old class ring from the bottom of her purse and tucked it under the inner pleat at the neckline of her blouse.

When Frank returned to her side he immediately placed his fingers on her throat and again Nora felt the tingling thrill she was learning to associate with parapsychological investigation. As she felt his hand gradually descend, however, she became apprehensive.

'What do you think you're doing?' she snapped.

'Why, looking for your ring,' Frank told her. 'It is a ring you concealed, isn't it?'

'Yes – but not *there*. It's up there, under the neckline.'

'That's where you intended to put it,' Frank answered, continuing his search. 'But it slipped down. In fact, quite a ways down. Don't worry, though, I'll get it.'

'It can't be *that* far down,' the girl protested.

'Oh, but it is. Hold still! Remember, this is just an experiment.'

Even controlled experiments can sometimes get out of hand, and this particular experiment rapidly became uncontrolled. There was no doubt in either of their minds, however, as to the experiment's success. Within two minutes Frank had found Nora's ring, and before another five minutes had elapsed, they were engaged to be married.

Since Dr. Angus Welk did not possess psi powers, he was quite blissfully unaware of his daughter's clandestine engagement. This situation seemed ideal to both Nora and Frank.

Their courtship was conducted in the park and at times in the last parking space at the rear of a drive-in movie. Since neither of them cared for motion pictures, they were free to continue their research into the super-normal, and Nora quickly graduated from the status of willing pupil to adoring convert, She soon learned that no matter what she hid nor where she hid it, Frank could seek it out unerringly. Just how long she might have continued as a subject for a wide field of investigation is problematical, had not an unforeseen crisis arisen.

The unforeseen crisis, in the person of Professor Seine, changed everything. The unforeseen Seine suddenly went off on a parapsychological wingding.

'It's murder, that's what it is!' Frank announced to Nora one late summer evening, after greeting her at the park entrance they had chosen for a trysting place. 'Did you see tonight's paper? Did your father tell you?'

She shook her head. 'No, I've just come from the office. Daddy stayed home all day today. What's the matter?'

'It's Seine. He's been grumbling about your father's attacks on him for months now. Says it's ridiculous that two men from the same university faculty should dispute with each other about a perfectly self-evident matter. And now he wants to bring the matter to a head. He issued a public challenge to your father today. Invited him to select a committee of six – anyone he wants – to witness a demonstration of parapsychological phenomena. He's coming to your father's house tomorrow with a subject, prepared to prove his case.'

'That's terrible,' the girl agreed. 'Daddy's going to be awfully upset.'

'He's not the only one,' Frank muttered. 'The subject Professor Seine selected for his demonstration happens to be me.'

'No – he couldn't!'

'He could, and he did. After all, I'm his star example. He wants to write this book about me, remember?'

'But why didn't you refuse?'

Frank paused and gulped.

'You could have refused,' Nora continued, relentlessly. 'Didn't we agree we'd keep our engagement a secret until you graduated, so Daddy would never know you were mixed up in these experiments? Didn't I tell you that he'd rather see me married to a psychopath than to a psychic sensitive? And didn't you promise me that you'd give up your investigations after you finished school and get an honest job in some laboratory where they do *real* psychological work – like ringing bells and teaching dogs to salivate?'

'Sure,' Frank answered. 'I wanted to make a good impression on your father. Approach him wearing a white smock and carrying a test tube full of Airedale saliva in one hand. But Professor Seine has convinced me, Nora. This work is important. If we can control ESP and psi powers it means the opening of a whole new era. Your father's a scientist. Surely, if we demonstrate the truth to him, he'll understand.'

Nora began to sniffle. 'He's a scientist, yes, but as you once remarked, he's also an old goat. Can't you understand? No matter what kind of proof you present, he won't believe it. He'll just hate you for it and then we'll never get married.' She sobbed aloud. 'I don't think you really want to marry me, anyway. You just like to have somebody around to experiment on.'

'That's not true, you know it isn't. I'm sure we're going to be married.' Frank spoke gravely. 'My super-normal percipience is never wrong. I've told you that sometimes I have these prophetic dreams, haven't I? And they always come true. Well, last night I had another. In this dream I saw you lying in bed. And you weren't alone.'

'Let's not be vulgar,' the girl murmured.

'What's vulgar about a baby?' Frank demanded. 'You were lying in bed with this newborn child. Cutest little thing you ever saw – looked just like me.'

'Boy or girl?' Nora asked, eagerly.

'That I can't tell you. The alarm rang and I woke up. You know how noises distract psi powers. Professor Seine has already warned your father about that – tomorrow's experiments must be conducted under fair conditions.'

Nora put her hands on his shoulders. 'You really intend to marry me, then,' she said, softly.

'Of course I do. And the dream proves it.'

'It proves something else, too, then,' the girl said. 'The experiments can't be conducted fairly.'

'What are you getting at?'

'Listen to me, now, I *know* Daddy. If you go to him and demonstrate your powers, he'll just flip. On the other hand, if you flop, he'll be delighted. He'll feel so good about proving his case that he'll agree to anything. I know this isn't the Dark Ages, darling – we could get married without his consent, any time we want. But I happen to love him too, even if he is an old goat. And I don't want to spend the rest of my life in the middle of a family quarrel.'

'Do you want to spend the rest of your life with a faker?' Frank snapped. 'As far as I'm concerned, we are in the Dark Ages, until we successfully demonstrate the unsuspected powers of the human mind. Now Professor Seine's theory—'

Nora stamped her foot. 'I wish Professor Seine would stick his theory in a pigeonhole and forget it! What I want to know, will you play along with me or won't you?'

'There's nothing I'd rather do,' said Frank, and meant it. 'But Nora, I just can't. Don't worry, things will work out anyway. I saw our baby in a dream—'

'As far as I'm concerned, that's the only place you'll ever see it,' Nora told him.

The girl turned and clattered out of the park. Frank sat down on a bench and groaned. He knew he was right. They *were* going to have a baby. But now he realized that it wasn't going to be accomplished through extrasensory perception.

Professor Etienne Seine whistled with Gallic gaiety as he piloted his Porsche in the direction of Dr. Welk's big house just outside of town. The Professor, despite his position as a member of the psychological *savant-garde*, had not developed any ESP powers of his own. Consequently it was some time before he noted the dejected air of the young man seated at his side.

'What is it that there is?' he inquired, solicitously. 'What sickens you? Is it that you dread the testing?'

Frank shook his head and attempted a reassuring smile. Evidently it was a failure, because Professor Seine continued to regard him quizzically.

'Is it that it is something you ate? Your stomach, she is upset?'

'My stomach, she is empty,' Frank told him.

'Ah, that is best, *mon brave*.' The Professor nodded gravely. 'As we well comprehend, the success of ESP or psi experimentation can be imperiled by physical distractions. Eating and drinking spoil the victory. What is that which the poet says? "There's many a slip between *coupe* and lip." But be of cheer, we shall not fail. We shall convince the Doctor Welk and his committee, we shall convince the reporters—'

'Reporters?' Frank groaned. 'Oh, no!'

'Oh, *oui*!' Professor Seine gestured ahead as they rounded the driveway leading to the Welk mansion. 'Regard them.'

Frank regarded the waiting figures grouped on the porch. He recognized several of Dr. Welk's colleagues on the faculty, plus two or three young men with the inevitable notebooks clustered around the corpulent red-faced man who scowled down at them over the rims of his glasses. A glimpse of Dr. Welk's eyes was enough to terrify Frank, until he realized their bulging prominence was due to a trick of the spectacle lenses. From their thickness, it was reasonable to assume they had been ground at Mount Palomar.

'*Myopique*,' the Professor murmured, apparently noting the same thing as he left the car and conducted Frank up the steps. 'But he will see much, today.'

Frank didn't answer. He was searching for a sight of Nora. The girl was not in evidence.

He hastily recalled himself to acknowledge introductions. In response to a question from one of the reporters, he enunciated his name slowly.

'Tallent,' the reporter repeated, as he scribbled. 'Didn't somebody write a book about you? Charles Fort, maybe?'

'Charles Fort was an old fool.' The rasping voice belonged to Dr. Welk. 'Except, of course, when he was young. Then he was a young fool.'

Professor Seine laughed merrily. 'It is this scepticism which we today shall overcome,' he predicted. 'If anyone advances anything new, people resist with all their might; they act as if they neither heard nor could comprehend; they speak of the new view with contempt, as if it were not worth the trouble of even so much as an investigation or a regard; and thus a new truth may wait a long time before it can make its way.'

'Just the kind of nonsense I expected from you,' Dr. Welk observed.

The Professor shrugged. 'This is not my nonsense,' he answered mildly. 'It is a statement of Goethe.'

'Humph, I might have known. Goethe was a fool, too. Very unsound. All you have to do is look at his prefrontal lobes.'

'This Gertie a friend of yours?' one of the reporters demanded, eagerly. But before the Professor could answer him, a disturbance was made by an appearance – and a very charming appearance it was in the form of Nora.

This form was duly admired as the young woman passed among the group and distributed glasses of a pink liquid.

'I thought you gentlemen might like a little refreshment before you began the tests,' she said.

'Hey, Bacardis!' exclaimed the reporter who wanted to know about Gertie.

The girl shook her head. 'No, it's only fruit punch.' She approached Frank and gave him a level stare. He started to open his mouth, but his throat went dry. Automatically he accepted a glass and drank. He wished now that Nora had stayed away. Her presence disturbed him greatly, and her aloofness disturbed him even more. He found it difficult to concentrate on what was going on.

Professor Seine had taken over now, and he was telling the reporters and Dr. Welk's committee a few things about tele-pathy, telekinesis, teleportation, clairvoyance, and dowsing. From a brief case he extracted a mimeographed report of his past six months of experimentation with Frank – the card-runs, the work with dice, the psychometric data.

Dr. Welk cleared his throat for action. 'Twaddle,' he said. 'Sheer twaddle. Nobody can read minds.' He strode over to Professor Seine. 'Go ahead and read my mind, I dare you to.' He glanced at his daughter. 'On second thought, maybe you'd better wait until Nora leaves. What I'm thinking about you is best not repeated in mixed company.'

'But I do not read of minds,' the Professor protested. 'It is the young man here. He is the sensitive.'

Frank smiled weakly. He didn't feel like a sensitive. He was numb. He watched Nora refill the glasses from a large pitcher and extended his own with an imploring look. Nora refused to meet his eyes. He couldn't tell what she was thinking. He couldn't – the realization came to him with a flash of horror – tell what *anyone* was thinking. His head was beginning to whirl.

'Let's go inside,' Dr. Welk was saying, 'and get this affair over with. I can't afford to waste much time with such tomfoolery – I've got a four o'clock appointment to trepan a gorilla.'

He led the party into a large old-fashioned study, with book-lined walls; obviously this was his private den in which he was wont to pace and growl at will.

'You'll find I have made the arrangements we agreed upon,' he told Professor Seine. 'As I understood it, you asked me to conceal a deck of cards somewhere within the room, and also a packet of letters—'

'Would you care for another drink before you begin?' Nora interrupted, coming in from the hall with a full pitcher. 'It's so hot today—'

'Sure,' said the reporter who had asked about Charles Fort. 'Say, you positive there isn't any liquor in this? Stuff tastes like it's got a kick in it.'

'Not at all,' Nora told him. 'As I understand it, liquor affects the precognitive faculties, doesn't it, Professor?'

'*Certainement*,' he responded. And as the company drank, Professor Seine proceeded to explain the theories he was about to demonstrate.

Frank tried again to concentrate upon the conversation, but everything was blurry. Nora's face wavered before him as she poured the contents of the pitcher into his glass. He tried to whisper to her. 'Darling, won't you at least say something to me? I'm so—'

But she had turned away, and now Professor Seine had his hand on Frank's shoulder and was propelling him to the table in the center of the room. He gestured at the crowd, indicating a row of chairs lined up against the far wall.

'And now, messieurs,' he began, 'if you will be so good as to discover your seats, we shall make a commencement. First we shall have the card-run, as I have explained. The doctor has undertaken to conceal a pack of playing cards here in this room. I shall now ask my subject to locate those cards.'

He turned to Frank expectantly. Frank stood there – conscious of the perspiration bathing his palms, and of nothing else. He couldn't concentrate. The room wavered. It was Nora's fault – she had deliberately upset him so that the experiment would be a failure. He glanced nervously at Professor Seine. The gaunt investigator looked at him trustingly. It would be terrible to let him down now. It would be terrible to let himself down. Dr. Welk was scowling, murmuring to the committee and the reporters.

Frank closed his eyes. Immediately the room steadied. He began to get a vague impression. It didn't come quickly or clearly, as such impressions usually did, but it was coming.

Eyes closed, he moved forward. One hand swept the line of bookcases. He fumbled for a book, removed it, reached behind.

From a space between the books and the wall he extracted a rectangular object. Opening his eyes, he gazed down at a package of playing cards.

His sigh of relief mingled with a sharp gasp from Dr. Welk.

'But that's not where I put them!' He exclaimed 'There must be some mistake—'

'Mistake?' Professor Seine smiled blandly as he took the unopened pack from Frank's hand. 'You concealed of the cards, did you not? And my subject found of the cards, did he not? Let us proceed to the experiment.'

Deftly he blindfolded Frank and placed him in the far corner of the room. Then, stepping briskly to the table, Professor Seine removed the pack, shuffled it, and extended it to the nearest committee member. Upon a whispered instruction, the committee member shuffled the pack again. A second committee member now laid the first card face down upon the table, in plain view.

Frank stood motionless.

'What do you perceive?' the Professor called.

Frank gulped. He clenched his fists.

'*Eh bien,* what it is that you see?' the Professor insisted.

Frank shuddered. 'Must I tell?' he quavered.

'But well sure, you must! Describe the card, please!!'

'All right,' Frank muttered. 'You asked for it. This card has the picture of a naked blonde lying on her back and kicking a heart in the air with both feet. I suppose it's the ace of hearts.'

As the crowd gasped, Frank raced on. 'And the second card, with the brunette and the pony, is the four of spades. The redhead and the sailor is the seven of diamonds, and the next one, with the three girls wearing the black brassières, is the nine of clubs—'

By this time Professor Seine was at the table, rapidly turning over the cards. Frank was right: the ace of hearts was followed, in turn, by the others as he'd described them.

'A wolf-pack, by George!' exclaimed one of the reporters, crowding up to the table. 'And boy, what a wolf-pack. Look at

20

this here queen of diamonds; how'd she get mixed up with the Jack? Hey, Doc, I didn't know you had anything like this around—'

'Neither did I,' muttered Dr. Welk. 'I mean, this is definitely not the deck I concealed. One of my students recently returned from a field expedition to Cuba. He brought back some curiosa for anthropological study and left them with me—'

'Yeah, sure,' said the reporter. 'We know how it is, Doc.' He tried to riffle through the rest of the deck, but Dr. Welk snatched it away. 'Perhaps we'd better get on with the next phase,' he said. 'We'll consider this sufficient evidence.'

'Ah, yes.' Professor Seine bowed blandly. 'There is now the matter of the letters.' He removed Frank's bandage, and in a low voice murmured, 'What departs?'

'Damned if I know,' Frank said. 'I think you'd better call it off. Everything's going blank again.'

'Here, have a drink.' Nora was at his elbow, extending a glass. Frank was about to wave it away until he realized she was smiling. He drank gratefully, although his throat burned. She passed around the room, refilling glasses.

Finally the Professor rapped for attention. 'My good colleague has been instructed to conceal some letters in this room. I shall now ask that the subject find these communiqués and read of them aloud to you.'

Frank shook his head. As he did so, the subliminal came to his aid. He walked waveringly to the desk, then paused. Dr. Welk's eyes narrowed, but as Frank moved away from the desk he gave a sigh of relief.

His bulging eyes widened again as Frank paused in front of a portrait of Whistler's Mother, then pushed it aside and began to manipulate the combination of a safe concealed behind the picture.

'That's not the place!' Dr. Welk shouted, rising. 'And how did you know the combination, anyway?'

Frank, moving as though in a trance, continued to twirl the dial. The safe swung open. Frank reached in and extracted a packet of letters, bound in faded red ribbons. He put his hand over them, his eyes closing.

'The first letter is dated June 12th, 1932,' he muttered. 'And it begins like this: Dear Honeybug, It is morning now but I can still taste your kisses. If only the nights would never end—'

'Give me those!' Dr. Welk snatched the bundle from his hand and stuffed it into his coat.

'Aren't you going to tell us if he's right, Doc?' cried the nearest reporter. 'What's with this "Honeybug" business?'

Dr. Welk's face blossomed with a sudden case of rubella. 'These are positively not the letters I had in mind,' he groaned. 'Professor Seine, what is the meaning of this? Are you making mock of me?'

'Non,' the parapsychologist protested. 'I do not make the mock of you.' He glanced nervously at Frank, who stood there goggling. 'We will commence the next phase of the experiment, please.' Professor Seine blinked and popped his hand to his mouth to stifle an expected belch. Several of the committee members noted the gesture and laughed raucously. Nora tittered in the background.

Professor Seine shrugged and made haste to continue. 'Dr. Welk has arranged certain objects in his lavatory, is it not?'

'It is certainly not,' Dr. Welk boomed. 'What I do in the lavatory is no concern of this investigation.'

'Why not, Doc?' asked the most persistent of the two reporters, lurching to his feet. 'Now take me, for instance. I do a lot of reading in the—'

'Kindly shut your trap!' shouted Dr. Welk. 'Professor Seine has reference to my laboratory. He asked me to arrange something on the table there, to test the subject's ESP powers.'

'Ah yes,' the Professor nodded. 'It is as I say, the laboratory in which the good doctor conducts of the experiments, and not the lavatory, in which the good doctor—'

'Get on with it!' yelled Dr. Welk. 'I'm stifling in here and I've got a splitting headache. I put some stuff out on the table.

Your stooge has never been in my laboratory. He's supposed to guess what's in there. Now, go ahead!'

Frank turned and put his palms to his forehead. He felt the room reel. His mouth opened, seemingly of its own volition. The words came. 'Reading from left to right,' he said, 'I see a series of jars. The first one contains dill pickles. The second one contains a pickled foetus. The third one contains pure water.'

He opened his eyes. 'That's right, isn't it?' he asked.

Dr. Welk nodded reluctantly. 'As far as it goes,' he conceded. 'But what about the fourth one?'

'Fourth one?' Frank frowned. 'There is no fourth one.'

'Oh yes there is,' Dr. Welk exclaimed triumphantly. 'Come along and I'll show you.'

The group trooped down the hall at Dr. Welk's heels. He moved slowly and seemed to have some difficulty opening the laboratory door. But once inside he gestured at the table with a flourish.

'You see?' he announced. 'Four jars!'

'Uh-uh,' said the eldest committee member. 'Six.'

'You're seeing double,' his nearest neighbor told him. 'There's only three.'

'Three!' echoed Professor Seine. '*Regardez donc!*'

'Four, in plain English!' contradicted Dr. Welk. Then he stared. 'Where'd it go?' he panted. 'Where'd it disappear to? I could have sworn I had a fourth jar there. It was filled with a gallon of medical alco—'

'Anyone for punch?' murmured Nora, sweetly, as she appeared in the doorway with a refilled pitcher.

Frank bore down upon her. He brushed her aside and whispered hastily, 'So that's it, that's what you did! Spiked punch! You knew I was affected by alcohol, you wanted to ruin the experiment. Well, I'll show you—'

But he had no time to show her anything. Professor Seine was leading them back along the hall, and out of the house.

'We conclude with the dowsing,' he said.

'Dowsing?' The reporter who knew Fort's name was instantly alert. 'That's where you find water with a forked stick, isn't it? But what's that got to do with psi?'

'It is an example of the clairvoyance, of a super-normal perceptive power,' Professor Seine told him, accepting a glass of punch. 'The willow wand, she is not necessary; she is mere superstition. *La radiesthésie* – that which you name the dowsing – can be accomplished as well with a bent coat hanger as you will quickly see.'

'Or just as poorly,' murmured Dr. Welk, lowering his voice so that Professor Seine could not hear him. 'I took the trouble to get some of the boys from the Geology Department over here. You'll find their reports inside. There's no water on my land anywhere – it's dry as a bone. Watch and see.'

Professor Seine, for his part, had collared the reporters, both of whom were accepting their fifth glass of punch from Nora.

'This instrument you observe on the lawn,' he explained. 'He is a portable well-digger I made rent of this morning. When my young friend discovers water, I shall avail myself of it to make the bore. Attend, he emanates from the house now with the coat hanger.'

Frank was emanating, but not very rapidly. A slow anger churned within him, mingling with the alcohol he had unwittingly consumed. Nora was giggling openly at him, but nobody seemed to notice it – the punch had done its work too well. Any attempt at extrasensory perception seemed doomed; for that matter nobody was in a condition to attempt normal perception. The side lawn was littered with straggling drunks as though a cocktail party had broken up and strewn the guests helter-skelter across the sward.

Dr. Welk was shouting incoherently at him and waving his arms. 'C'mon, let's finish this up!' he called. 'Don't forget, I've got a four o'clock date with a gorilla!'

'This is not of the time for monkey business,' Professor Seine retorted. 'I ask that you be silent as the grave. The subject must concentrate with the utmost.'

Frank raised the coat hanger. He took a deep breath, hoping to restore his sobriety. He had found water before; if there was a trace of moisture anywhere on this land, he knew the forces within him would inevitably lead him to it. The coat hanger would jerk, then point. And Professor Seine would drill. The Professor stalked behind him, panting now as he lifted the heavy portable driller with its long electrical cord trailing behind from its extension plug-in back at the house. The cord was three hundred feet long. Frank began to walk, slowly, his head bent.

'Stop!' murmured the professor. 'The cord, she is at the end of her rope.'

Frank retraced his steps. The coat hanger remained steadily outstretched before him. The crowd trailed behind, stumbling and giggling. Suddenly Frank wheeled abruptly and started for the house. He halted just under one of the bay windows and the coat hanger jerked down as if independently directed.

'Here,' Frank whispered.

Professor Seine began to rig his drill.

'No!' Dr. Welk protested. 'No, there isn't any water! I've had the place inspected, there can't be! Don't ruin my flowerbeds – don't you dare turn that thing on – stop him, somebody!'

But as the group converged on Frank and the professor, the drill went into action. There was a whirring, a piercing of soft earth. And then—

A wave of water spurted upwards, then fell in a flashing arc to drench the crowd.

A geyser spouted from the sod.

Frank beamed at the girl.

'I did it!' he cried.

'*Sacre!*' ejaculated the professor. '*Sacre du printemps!*'

'Look!' Frank grabbed Nora and shook her, holding her under the spray. 'He's got to believe me now, doesn't he! I can do anything, liquor or no liquor. I can produce apports, poltergeists, phenomena, anything. I've got the power, see? I can levitate, teleport – just you watch me—'

'You damned fool!' Dr. Welk staggered over. 'Know what you just did? *You hit the city water main!*'

Professor Seine was frantically tugging at the drill. 'It is immovable,' he gasped. 'I cannot extricate it—'

'Here, let me try!' Frank tugged at it, then turned. 'Never mind, I'll levitate it.' He faced the drenched and leaping crowd. 'Now watch!' he yelled. 'I'll prove I have psi powers once and for all – look at this!'

He allowed the darkness to surge over him, the blurry, alcoholic darkness. With his inner eye he could see the drill rising out of the ground as if of its own accord. He could see it lifting higher and higher. He strained to elevate it, watched it twirl above his head, and then the effort was too much. It was dropping, coming closer and closer. Frank tried to dodge, but he was too late. As the shrieking committee scattered in all directions, the drill landed on Frank's head and the darkness closed in.

It took ten stitches to patch up his skull, but Nora patched up the rest. Before the sobered, sodden committee left the house they had agreed to keep silence on the entire affair – including their own part in it. Perhaps Nora's admission about the spiked punch helped. At any rate, no one was willing to go on record as having participated in the debacle. As for the reporters, neither of them was inclined to turn in a story.

'Who'd believe it anyway?' said the one who was interested in Fort. 'My city editor's death on that kind of stuff. He wouldn't recognize a flying saucer if his wife hit him with one.'

Professor Seine was happy, however. In his eyes the experiment was a complete success, and once he was assured Frank's injury wasn't serious, he even agreed to pay for the cost of repairing the damaged water main.

Dr. Welk's reaction was curiously complex. He had seen enough to modify his attitude on parapsychology – but at the same time he had his reputation to consider. Fortunately, as

Nora pointed out, no one would know. She certainly wouldn't say anything, and neither would Frank.

The young man didn't learn all this until later. He sat up in bed at the hospital and listened to Nora's account.

'So you see, it all worked out for the best,' she told him. 'Daddy isn't angry at you for what happened. He feels you saved him, really.'

'*I* saved him?'

Nora blushed. 'Yes, I told him it was your idea to spike the punch that way.'

'But, darling—'

'Don't you see? It's all right now. We can be married, and you can continue your experiments in private, if you want.'

'No I can't.' Frank's tone was sepulchral.

'What do you mean?'

'That blow on the head. It did something to me. I – I've been testing. The power doesn't work any more. I can't tell what's written on my chart, and I don't even know what you have in your purse.'

Nora sighed. 'I don't know whether I'm happy or sad,' she said, reaching for his hand. 'But don't worry. Maybe it will come back when you're well again.'

She was wrong, of course. It didn't come back. And some nine months after they were married – and Frank had an excellent job as assistant to Dr. Welk, cataloguing the pelvic bones of Australian aborigines – came the fatal hour.

As the young man paced the floor outside the delivery room, a nurse asked him the usual question. 'Which do you think it will be?' she inquired. 'Boy or girl?'

'Damned if I know,' Frank groaned. 'What do you think I am – a mind-reader?'

COMFORT ME, MY ROBOT

When Henson came in, the Adjustor was sitting inside his desk, telescreening a case. At the sound of the doortone he flicked a switch. The posturchair rose from the center of the desk until the Adjustor's face peered at the visitor from an equal level.

'Oh, it's you,' said the Adjustor.

'Didn't the girl tell you? I'm here to see you professionally.'

If the Adjustor was surprised, he didn't show it. He cocked a thumb at the posturchair. 'Sit down and tell me all about it, Henson,' he said.

'Nothing to tell.' Henson stared out of the window at the plains of Upper Mongolia. 'It's just a routine matter. I'm here to make a request and you're the Adjustor.'

'And your request is—?'

'Simple,' said Henson. 'I want to kill my wife.'

The Adjustor nodded. 'That can be arranged,' he murmured. 'Of course, it will take a few days.'

'I can wait.'

'Would Friday be convenient?'

'Good enough. That way it won't cut into my weekend. Lita and I were planning a fishing trip, up New Zealand way. Care to join us?'

'Sorry, but I'm tied up until Monday.' The Adjustor stifled a yawn. 'Why do you want to kill Lita?' he asked.

'She's hiding something from me.'

'What do you suspect?'

'That's just it – I don't know what to suspect. And it keeps bothering me.'

'Why don't you question her?'

'Violation of privacy. Surely you, as a certified public Adjustor, wouldn't advocate that?'

'Not professionally.' The Adjustor grinned. 'But since we're personal friends, I don't mind telling you that there are times when I think privacy should be violated. This notion of individual rights can become a fetish.'

'Fetish?'

'Just an archaism.' The Adjustor waved a casual dismissal to the word. He leaned forward. 'Then, as I understand it, your wife's attitude troubles you. Rather than embarrass her with questions, you propose to solve the problem delicately, by killing her.'

'Right.'

'A very chivalrous attitude, I admire it.'

'I'm not sure whether I do or not,' Henson mused. 'You see, it really wasn't my idea. But the worry was beginning to affect my work, and my Administrator – Loring, you know him, I believe – took me aside for a talk. He suggested I see you and arrange for a murder.'

'Then it's to be murder.' The Adjustor frowned. 'You know, actually, we are supposed to be the arbiters when it comes to method. In some cases a suicide works just as well. Or an accident.'

'I want a murder,' Henson said. 'Premeditated, and in the first degree.' Now it was his turn to grin. 'You see, I know a few archaisms myself.'

The Adjustor made a note. 'As long as we're dealing in archaic terminology, might I characterize your attitude towards your wife as one of – jealousy?'

Henson controlled his blush at the sound of the word. He nodded slowly. 'I guess you're right,' he admitted. 'I can't bear the idea of her having any secrets. I know it's immature and absurd, and that's why I'm seeking an immature solution.'

'Let me correct you,' said the Adjustor. 'Your solution is far from immature. A good murder probably is the most adult approach to your problem. After all, man, this is the twenty-second century, not the twentieth. Although even way back then they were beginning to learn some of the answers.'

'Don't tell me they had Adjustors,' Henson murmured.

'No, of course not. In those days this field was only a small, neglected part of physical medicine. Practitioners were called psychiatrists, psychologists, auditors, analysts – and a lot of other things. That was their chief stock in trade, by the way: name-calling and labelling.'

The Adjustor gestured toward the slide-files. 'I must have five hundred spools transcribed there,' he calculated. 'All of it from books – nineteenth, twentieth, even early twenty-first century material. And it's largely terminology, not technique. Psychotherapy was just like alchemy in those days. Everything was named and defined. Inability to cope with environment was minutely broken down into hundreds of categories, thousands of terms. There were "schools" of therapy, with widely divergent theories and applications. And the crude attempts at technique they used – you wouldn't believe it unless you studied what I have here! Everything from trying to "cure" a disorder in one session by means of brain-surgery or electric shock to the other extreme of letting the "patient" talk about his problems for thousands of hours over a period of years.'

He smiled. 'I'm afraid I'm letting my personal enthusiasm run away with me. After all, Henson, you aren't interested in the historical aspects. But I did have a point I wanted to make. About the maturity of murder as a solution-concept.'

Henson adjusted the posturchair as he listened.

'As I said, even back in the twentieth century, they were beginning to get a hint of the answer. It was painfully apparent that some of the techniques I mention weren't working at all. "Sublimation" and "catharsis" helped but did not cure in a majority of cases. Physical therapy altered and warped the personality. And all the while, the answer lay right before their eyes.

'Let's take your twentieth-century counterpart for an

example. Man named Henson, who was jealous of his wife. He might go to an analyst for years without relief. Whereas if he did the sensible thing, he'd take an axe to her and kill her.

'Of course, in the twentieth century such a procedure was antisocial and illegal. Henson would be sent to prison for the rest of his life.

'But the chances are, he'd function perfectly thereafter. Having relieved his psychic tension by the commonsense method of direct action, he'd have no further difficulty in adjustment.

'Gradually the psychiatrists observed this phenomenon. They learned to distinguish between the psychopath and the perfectly normal human being who sought to relieve an intolerable situation. It was hard, because once a normal man was put in prison, he was subject to new tensions and stresses which caused fresh aberrations. But these aberrations stemmed from his confinement – not from the impulse which led him to kill.' Again the Adjustor paused. 'I hope I'm not making this too abtruse for you,' he said. 'Terms like "psychopath" and "normal" can't have much meaning to a layman.'

'I understand what you're driving at,' Henson told him. 'Go ahead. I've always wondered how Adjustment evolved, anyway.'

'I'll make it brief from now on,' the Adjustor promised. 'The next crude step was something called the "psycho-drama". It was a simple technique in which an aberrated individual was encouraged to get up on a platform, before an audience, and act out his fantasies – including those involving aggression and violently anti-social impulses. This afforded great relief. Well, I won't trouble you with the historical details about the establishment of Master Control, right after North America went under in the Blast. We got it, and the world started afresh, and one of the groups set up was Adjustment. All of physical medicine, all of what was then called sociology and psychiatry, came under the scope of this group. And from that point on we started to make real progress.

'Adjustors quickly learned that old-fashioned therapies must be discarded. Naming or classifying a mental disturbance didn't necessarily overcome it. Talking about it, distracting attention from it, teaching the patient a theory about it, were not solutions. Nor was chopping out or shocking out part of his brain structure.

'More and more we came to rely on direct action as a cure, just as we do in physical medicine.

'Then, of course, robotics came along and gave us the final answer. And it is the answer, Henson – that's the thought I've been trying to convey. Because we're friends, I know you well enough to eliminate all the preliminaries. I don't have to give you a battery of tests, check reactions, and go through the other formalities. But if I did, I'm sure I'd end up with the same answer – in your case, the mature solution is to murder your wife as quickly as possible. That will cure you.'

'Thanks,' said Henson. 'I knew I could count on you.'

'No trouble at all.' The Adjustor stood up. He was a tall, handsome man with curly red hair, and he somewhat towered over Henson who was only six feet and a bit too thin.

'You'll have papers to sign, of course,' the Adjustor reminded him. 'I'll get everything ready by Friday morning. If you'll step in then, you can do it in ten minutes.'

'Fine.' Henson smiled. 'Then I think I'll plan the murder for Friday evening, at home. I'll get Lita to visit her mother in Saigon overnight. Best if she doesn't know about this until afterwards.'

'Thoughtful of you,' the Adjustor agreed. 'I'll have her robot requisitioned for you from Inventory. Any special requirements?'

'I don't believe so. It was made less than two years ago, and it's almost a perfect match. Paid almost seven thousand for the job.'

'That's a lot of capital to destroy.' The Adjustor sighed. 'Still it's necessary. Will you want anything else – weapons, perhaps?'

'No.' Henson stood in the doorway. 'I think I'll just strangle her.'

'Very well, then. I'll have the robot here and operating for you on Friday morning. And you'll take your robot too.'

'Mine? Why, might I ask?'

'Standard procedure. You see, we've learned something more about the mind – about what used to be called a "guilt complex". Sometimes a man isn't freed by direct action alone. There may be a peculiar desire for punishment involved. In the old days many men who committed actual murders had this need to be caught and punished. Those who avoided capture frequently punished themselves. They developed odd psychosomatic reactions – some even committed suicide.

'In case you have any such impulses, your robot will be available to you. Punish it any way you like – destroy it, if necessary. That's the sensible thing to do.'

'Right. See you Friday morning, then. And many thanks.' Henson started through the doorway. He looked back and grinned. 'You know, just thinking about it makes me feel better already!'

Henson whizzed back to the Adjustor's office on Friday morning. He was in rare good humor all the way. Anticipation was a wonderful thing. Everything was wonderful, for that matter.

Take robots, for example. The simple, uncomplicated mechanisms did all the work, all the drudgery. Their original development for military purposes during the twenty-first century was forgotten now, along with the concept of war which had inspired their creation. Now the automatons functioned as workers.

And for the well-to-do there were these personalized surrogates. What a convenience!

Henson remembered how he'd argued to convince Lita they should invest in a pair when they married. He'd used all of the sensible modern arguments. 'You know as well as I do what having them will save us in terms of time and efficiency. We

33

can send them to all the boring banquets and social functions. They can represent us at weddings and funerals, that sort of thing. After all, it's being done everywhere nowadays. Nobody attends such affairs in person any more if they can afford not to. Why, you see them on the street everywhere. Remember Kirk, at our reception? Stayed four hours, life of the party and everybody was fooled – you didn't know it was his robot until he told you.'

And so forth, on and on. 'Aren't you sentimental at all darling? If I died wouldn't you like to have my surrogate around to comfort you? I certainly would want yours to share the rest of my life.'

Yes, he'd used all the practical arguments except the psychotherapeutic one – at that time it had never occurred to him. But perhaps it should have, when he heard her objections.

'I just don't like the idea,' Lita had persisted. 'Oh it isn't that I'm old-fashioned. But lying there in the forms having every detail of my body duplicated synthetically – ugh! And then they do that awful hypnotherapy or whatever it's called for days to make them think. Oh I know they have no brains, it's only a lot of chemicals and electricity, but they do duplicate your thought patterns and they react the same and they sound so real. I don't want anyone or anything to know all my secrets—'

Yes that objection should have started him thinking. Lita had secrets even then.

But he'd been too busy to notice; he'd spent his efforts in battering down her objections. And finally she'd consented.

He remembered the days at the Institute – the tests they'd taken, the time spent in working with the anatomists, the cosmetic department, the sonic and visio adaptors, and then days of hypnotic transference.

Lita was right in a way; it hadn't been pleasant. Even a modern man was bound to feel a certain atavistic fear when confronted for the first time with his completed surrogate. But the finished product was worth it. And after Henson had mastered instructions, learned how to manipulate the robot by virtue of the control-command, he had been almost paternally proud of the creation.

He'd wanted to take his surrogate home with him, but Lita positively drew the line at that.

'We'll leave them both here in Inventory,' she said. 'If we need them we can always send for them. But I hope we never do.'

Henson was finally forced to agree. He and Lita had both given their immobilization commands to the surrogates, and they were placed in their metal cabinets ready to be filed away – 'Just like corpses!' Lita had shuddered. 'We're looking at ourselves after we're dead.'

And that had ended the episode. For a while, Henson made suggestions about using the surrogates – there were occasions he'd have liked to take advantage of a substitute for token public appearances – but Lita continued to object. And so, for two years now, the robots had been on file. Henson paid his taxes and fees on them annually and that was all.

That was all, until lately. Until Lita's unexplained silences and still more inexplicable absences had started Henson thinking. Thinking and worrying. Worrying and watching. Watching and waiting. Waiting to catch her, waiting to kill her—

So he'd remembered psychotherapy, and had gone to his Adjustor. Lucky the man was a friend of his; a friend of both of them, rather. Actually, Lita had known him longer than her husband. But they'd been very close, the three of them, and he knew the Adjustor would understand.

He could trust the Adjustor not to tell Lita. He could trust the Adjustor to have everything ready and waiting for him now.

Henson went up to the office. The papers were ready for him to sign. The two metal boxes containing the surrogates were already placed on the loaders ready for transport to wherever he designated. But the Adjustor wasn't on hand to greet him.

'Special assignment in Manila,' the Second explained to him. 'But he left instructions about your case, Mr. Henson. All you have to do is sign the responsibility slips. And of course, you'll be in Monday for the official report.'

Henson nodded. Now that the moment was so near at hand he was impatient of details. He could scarcely wait until the micro-dupes were completed and the Register Board signalled clearance. Two common robots were requisitioned to carry the metal cases down to the gyro and load them in. Henson whizzed back home with them and they brought the cases up to his living-level. Then he dismissed them, and he was alone.

He was alone. He could open the cases now. First, his own. He slid back the cover, gazed down at the perfect duplicate of his own body, sleeping peacefully for two serene years since its creation. Henson stared curiously at his pseudo-countenance. He'd aged a bit in two years, but the surrogate was ageless. It could survive the ravage of centuries, and it was always at peace. Always at peace. He almost envied it. The surrogate didn't love, couldn't hate, wouldn't know the gnawing torture of suspicion that led to this shaking, quaking, aching lust to kill—

Henson shoved the lid back and lifted the metal case upright, then dragged it along the wall to a storage cabinet. A domestic-model could have done it for him, but Lita didn't like domestic-models. She wouldn't permit even a common robot in her home.

Lita and her likes and dislikes! Damn her and them too!

Henson ripped the lid down on the second file.

There she was; the beautiful, harlot-eyed, blonde, lying, adorable, dirty, gorgeous, loathsome, heavenly, filthy little goddess of a slut!

He remembered the command word to awake her. It almost choked him now but he said it.

'Beloved!'

Nothing happened. Then he realized why. He'd been almost snarling. He had to change the pitch of his voice. He tried again, softly. 'Beloved!'

She moved. Her breasts rose and fell, rose and fell. She

opened her eyes. She held out her arms and smiled. She stood up and came close to him, without a word.

Henson stared at her. She was newly-born and innocent, she had no secrets, she wouldn't betray him. How could he harm her? How could he harm her when she lifted her face in expectation of a kiss?

But she was Lita. He had to remember that. She was Lita, and Lita was hiding something from him and she must be punished, would be punished.

Suddenly, Henson became conscious of his hands. There was a tingling in his wrists and it ran down through the strong muscles and sinews to the fingers, and the fingers flexed and unflexed with exultant vigor, and then they rose and curled around the surrogate's throat, around Lita's throat, and they were squeezing and squeezing and the surrogate, Lita, tried to move away and the scream was almost real and the popping eyes were almost real and the purpling face was almost real, only nothing was real any more except the hands and the choking and the surging sensation of strength.

And then it was over. He dragged the limp, dangling mechanism (it was only a mechanism now, just as the hate was only a memory) to the waste-jet and fed the surrogate to the flame. He turned the aperture wide and thrust the metal case in, too.

Then Henson slept, and he did not dream. For the first time in months he did not dream, because it was over and he was himself again. The therapy was complete.

'So that's how it was.' Henson sat in the Adjustor's office, and the Monday morning sun was strong on his face.

'Good.' The Adjustor smiled and ran a hand across the top of his curly head. 'And how did you and Lita enjoy your weekend? Fish biting?'

'We didn't fish,' said Henson. 'We talked.'

'Oh?'

'I figured I'd have to tell her what happened, sooner or later. So I did.'

'How did she take it?'

'Very well, at first.'

'And then—?'

'I asked her some questions.'

'Yes.'

'She answered them.'

'You mean she told you what she'd been hiding?'

'Not willingly. But she told me. After I told her about my own little check-up.'

'What was that?'

'I did some calling Friday night. She wasn't in Saigon with her mother.'

'No?'

'And you weren't in Manila on a special case, either.' Henson leaned forward. 'The two of you were together, in New Singapore! I checked it and she admitted it.'

The Adjustor sighed. 'So now you know,' he said.

'Yes. Now I know. Now I know what she's been concealing from me. What you've both been concealing.'

'Surely you're not jealous about that?' the Adjustor asked. 'Not in this modern day and age when—'

'She says she wants to have a child by you,' Henson said. 'She refused to bear one for me. But she wants yours. She told me so.'

'What do you want to do about it?' the Adjustor asked.

'You tell me,' Henson murmured. 'That's why I've come to you. You're my Adjustor.'

'What would you like to do?'

'I'd like to kill you,' Henson said. 'I'd like to blow off the top of your head with a pocket-blast.'

'Not a bad idea.' The Adjustor nodded. 'I'll have my robot ready whenever you say.'

'At my place,' said Henson. 'Tonight.'

'Good enough. I'll send it there to you.'

'One thing more.' Henson gulped for a moment. 'In order for it to do any good, Lita must watch.'

It was the Adjustor's turn to gulp, now. 'You mean you're going to force her to see you go through with this?'

'I told her and she agreed,' Henson said.

'But, think of the effect on her, man!'

'Think of the effect on me. Do you want me to go mad?'

'No,' said the Adjustor. 'You're right. It's therapy. I'll send the robot around at eight. Do you need a pocket-blast requisition?'

'I have one,' said Henson.

'What instructions shall I give my surrogate?' the Adjustor asked.

Henson told him. He was brutally explicit, and midway in his statement the Adjustor looked away, coloring. 'So the two of you will be together, just as if you were real, and then I'll come in and—'

The Adjustor shuddered a little, then managed a smile. 'Sound therapy,' he said. 'If that's the way you want it, that's the way it will be.'

That's the way Henson wanted it, and that's the way he had it – up to a point.

He burst into the room around quarter after eight and found the two of them waiting for him. There was Lita, and there was the Adjustor's surrogate. The surrogate had been well-instructed; it looked surprised and startled. Lita needed no instruction; hers was an agony of shame.

Henson had the pocket-blast in his hand, cocked at the ready. He aimed.

Unfortunately, he was just a little late. The surrogate sat up gracefully and slid one hand under the pillow. The hand came up with another pocket-blast aimed and fired all in one motion.

Henson teetered, tottered, and fell. The whole left side of his face sheared away as he went down.

Lita screamed.

Then the surrogate put his arms around her and whispered, 'It's all over, darling. All over. We did it! He really thought I

39

was a robot, that I'd go through with his aberrated notion of dramatizing his revenge.'

The Adjustor smiled and lifted her face to his. 'From now on you and I will always be together. We'll have our child, lots of children if you wish. There's nothing to come between us now.'

'But you killed him,' Lita whispered. 'What will they do to you?'

'Nothing. It was self-defense. Don't forget, I'm an Adjustor. From the moment he came into my office, everything he did or said was recorded during our interviews. The evidence will show that I tried to humor him, that I indicated his mental unbalance and allowed him to work out his own therapy.

'This last interview, today, will not be a part of the record. I've already destroyed it. So as far as the law is concerned, he had no grounds for jealousy or suspicion. I happened to stop in here to visit this evening and found him trying to kill you – the actual you. And when he turned on me, I blasted him in self-defense.'

'Will you get away with it?'

'Of course I'll get away with it. The man was aberrated, and the record will show it.'

The Adjustor stood up. 'I'm going to call Authority now,' he said.

Lita rose and put her hand on his shoulders. 'Kiss me first,' she whispered. 'A real kiss. I like real things.'

'Real things,' said the Adjustor. She snuggled against him, but he made no move to take her in his arms. He was staring down at Henson.

Lita followed his gaze.

Both of them saw it at the same time, then – both of them saw the torn hole in the left side of Henson's head, and the thin strands of wire protruding from the opening.

'He didn't come,' the Adjustor murmured. 'He must have suspected, and he sent his robot instead.'

Lita began to shake. 'You were to send your robot, but you

didn't. He was to come himself, but he sent his robot. Each of you double-crossed the other, and now—'

And now the door opened very quickly.

Henson came into the room.

He looked at his surrogate lying on the floor. He looked at Lita. He looked at the Adjustor. Then he grinned. There was no madness in his grin, only deliberation.

There was deliberation in the way he raised the pocket-blast. He aimed well and carefully, fired only once, but both the Adjustor and Lita crumpled in the burst.

Henson bent over the bodies, inspecting them carefully to make sure that they were real. He was beginning to appreciate Lita's philosophy now. He liked real things.

For that matter, the Adjustor had some good ideas, too. This business of dramatizing aggressions really seemed to work. He didn't feel at all angry or upset any more, just perfectly calm and at peace with the world.

Henson rose, smiled, and walked towards the door. For the first time in years he felt completely adjusted.

TALENT

It is perhaps a pity that nothing is known of Andrew Benson's parents.

The same reasons which prompted them to leave him as a foundling on the steps of the St. Andrews Orphanage also caused them to maintain a discreet anonymity. The event occurred on the morning of March 3rd, 1943 – the war era, as you probably recall – so in a way the child may be regarded as a wartime casualty. Similar occurrences were by no means rare during those days, even in Pasadena, where the Orphanage was located.

After the usual tentative and fruitless inquiries, the good Sisters took him in. It was there that he acquired his first name, from the patron and patronymic saint of the establishment. The 'Benson' was added some years later, by the couple who eventually adopted him.

It is difficult at this late date, to determine what sort of a child Andrew was; orphanage records are sketchy, at best, and Sister Rosemarie, who acted as supervisor of the boys' dormitory is long since dead. Sister Albertine, the primary grades teacher of the Orphanage School, is now – to put it as delicately as possible – in her senility, and her testimony is necessarily colored by knowledge of subsequent events.

That Andrew never learned to talk until he was nearly seven years old seems almost incredible; the forced gregarity and the conspicuous lack of individual attention characteristic of orphanage upbringing would make it appear as though the ability to speak is necessary for actual survival in such an environment from infancy onward. Scarcely more credible is Sister Albertine's theory that Andrew knew how to talk but merely refused to do so until he was well into his seventh year.

For what it is worth, she now remembers him as an unusually precocious youngster, who appeared to possess an intelligence and understanding far beyond his years. Instead of employing speech, however, he relied on pantomime, an art at which he was so brilliantly adept (if Sister Albertine is to be believed) that his continuing silence seemed scarcely noticeable.

'He could imitate anybody,' she declares. 'The other children, the Sisters, even the Mother Superior. Of course I had to punish him for that. But it was remarkable, the way he was able to pick up all the little mannerisms and facial expressions of another person, just at a glance. And that's all it took for Andrew – just a mere glance.

'Visitors' Day was Sunday. Naturally, Andrew never had any visitors, but he liked to hang around the corridor and watch them come in. And afterwards, in the dormitory at night, he'd put in a regular performance for the other boys. He could impersonate every single man, woman or child who'd come to the Orphanage that day – the way they walked, the way they moved, every action and gesture. Even though he never said a word, nobody made the mistake of thinking Andrew was mentally deficient. For a while, Dr. Clement had the idea he might be a mute.'

Dr. Roger Clement is one of the few persons who might be able to furnish more objective data concerning Andrew Benson's early years. Unfortunately, he passed away in 1954; a victim of a fire which also destroyed his home and his office files.

It was Dr. Clement who attended Andrew on the night that he saw his first motion picture.

The date was 1949, some Saturday evening in the late fall of the year. The Orphanage received and showed one film a week, and only children of school age were permitted to attend. Andrew's inability – or unwillingness – to speak had caused some difficulty when he entered primary grades that

43

September, and several months went by before he was allowed to join his classmates in the auditorium for the Saturday night screenings. But it is known that he eventually did so.

The picture was the last (and probably the least) of the Marx Brothers movies. Its title was *Love Happy*, and if it is remembered by the general public at all today, that is due to the fact that the film contained a brief walk-on appearance by a then-unknown blonde bit player named Marilyn Monroe.

But the Orphanage audience had other reasons for regarding it as memorable. Because *Love Happy* was the picture that sent Andrew Benson into his trance.

Long after the lights came up again in the auditorium the child sat there, immobile, his eyes staring glassily at the blank screen. When his companions noticed and sought to arouse him he did not respond; one of the Sisters (possibly Sister Rosemarie) shook him, and he promptly collapsed in a dead faint. Dr. Clement was summoned, and he administered to the patient. Andrew Benson did not recover consciousness until the following morning.

And it was then that he talked.

He talked immediately, he talked perfectly, he talked fluently – but not in the manner of a six-year-old child. The voice that issued from his lips was that of a middle-aged man. It was a nasal, rasping voice, and even without the accompanying grimaces and facial expressions it was instantaneously and unmistakably recognizable as the voice of Groucho Marx.

Andrew Benson mimicked Groucho in his *Sam Grunion* role to perfection, word for word. Then he 'did' Chico Marx. After that he relapsed into silence again, and for a moment it was thought he had reverted to his mute phase. But it was an eloquent silence, and soon it became evident that he was imitating Harpo. In rapid succession, Andrew created recognizable vocal and visual portraits of Raymond Burr, Melville Cooper, Eric Blore and the other actors who played small roles in the picture. His impersonations seemed uncanny to his companions, and the Sisters were not unimpressed.

44

'Why, he even *looked* like Groucho,' Sister Albertine insists.

Ignoring the question of how a towheaded moppet of six can achieve a physical resemblance to Groucho Marx without benefit (or detriment) of make-up, it is nevertheless an established fact that Andrew Benson gained immediate celebrity as a mimic within the small confines of the Orphanage.

And from that moment on, he talked regularly, if not freely. That is to say, he replied to direct questions, he recited his lessons in the classroom, and responded with the outward forms of politeness required by Orphanage discipline. But he was never loquacious, or even communicative, in the ordinary sense. The only time he became spontaneously articulate was immediately following the showing of a weekly movie.

There was no recurrence of his initial seizure, but each Saturday night screening brought in its wake a complete dramatic recapitulation by the gifted youngster. During the fall of '49 and the winter of '50, Andrew Benson saw many movies. There was *Sorrowful Jones*, with Bob Hope; *Tarzan's Magic Fountain; the Fighting O'Flynn; The Life of Riley; Little Women*, and a number of other films, current and older. Naturally, these pictures were subject to approval by the Sisters before being shown, and as a result movies depicting or emphasizing violence were not included. Still, several Westerns reached the Orphanage screen, and it is significant that Andrew Benson reacted in what was to become a characteristic fashion.

'Funny thing,' declares Albert Dominguez, who attended the Orphanage during the same period as Andrew Benson and is one of the few persons located who is willing to admit, let alone discuss the fact. 'At first Andy imitated everybody – all the men, that is. He never imitated none of the women. But after he started to see Westerns, it got so he was choosey, like. He just imitated the villains. I don't mean like when us guys was playing cowboys – you know, when one guy is the Sheriff and one is a gun-slinger. I mean he imitated villains all the time. He could talk like 'em, he could even look like 'em. We used to razz hell out of him, you know?'

It is probably as a result of the 'razzing' that Andrew Benson, on the evening of May 17th, 1950, attempted to slit the throat of Frank Phillips with a table-knife. Probably – although Albert Dominguez claims that the older boy offered no provocation, and that Andrew Benson was exactly duplicating the screen role of a western desperado in an old Charles Starrett movie.

The incident was hushed up, apparently, and no action taken; we have little information on Andrew Benson's growth and development between the summer of 1950 and the autumn of 1955. Dominguez left the orphanage, nobody else appears willing to testify, and Sister Albertine had retired to a rest-home. As a result, there is nothing available concerning what may well have been Andrew's crucial, formative years. The meager records of his class-work seem satisfactory enough, and there is nothing to indicate that he was a disciplinary problem to his instructors. In June of 1955 he was photographed with the rest of his classmates upon the occasion of graduation from eighth grade. His face is a mere blur, an almost blank smudge in a sea of pre-adolescent countenances. What he actually looked like at that age is hard to tell.

The Bensons thought that he resembled their son, David.

Little David Benson had died of polio in 1953, and two years later his parents came to St. Andrews Orphanage seeking to adopt a boy. They had David's picture with them, and they were frank to state that they sought a physical resemblance as a guide to making their choice.

Did Andrew Benson see that photograph? Did – as has been subsequently theorized by certain irresponsible alarmists – he see certain *home movies* which the Bensons had taken of their child?

We must confine ourselves to the known facts, which are, simply, that Mr. and Mrs. Louis Benson, of Pasadena, California, legally adopted Andrew Benson, aged 12, on December 9th, 1955.

And Andrew Benson went to live in their home, as their son.

He entered the public high school. He became the owner of a bicycle. He received an allowance of one dollar a week. And he went to the movies.

Andrew Benson went to the movies, and there were no restrictions. No restrictions at all. For several months, that is. During this period he saw comedies, dramas, Westerns, musicals, melodramas. He must have seen melodramas. Was there a film, released early in 1956, in which an actor played the role of a gangster who pushed a victim out of a second-story window?

Knowing what we do today, we must suspect that there must have been. But at the time, when the actual incident occurred, Andrew Benson was virtually exonerated. He and the other boy had been 'scuffling' in a classroom after school, and the boy had 'accidentally fallen'. At least, this is the official version of the affair. The boy – now Pvt. Raymond Schuyler, USMC – maintains to this day that Benson deliberately tried to kill him.

'He was spooky, that kid,' Schuyler insists. 'None of us ever really got close to him. It was like there was nothing to get close to, you know? I mean, he kept changing off so. From one day to the next you could never figure out what he was going to be like. Of course we all knew he imitated these movie actors – he was only a freshman but already he was a big shot in the dramatic club – but it was as though he imitated all the time. One minute he'd be real quiet, and the next, wham! You know that story, the one about Jekyll and Hyde? Well, that was Andrew Benson. Afternoon he grabbed me, we weren't even talking to each other. He just came up to me at the window and I swear to God he changed right before my eyes. It was as if he all of a sudden got about a foot taller and fifty pounds heavier, and his face was real wild. He pushed me out of the window, without one word. Of course I was scared spitless, and maybe I just thought he changed. I mean, nobody can actually do a thing like that, can they?'

This question, if it arose at all at the time, remained unanswered. We do know that Andrew Benson was brought to the attention of Dr. Max Fahringer, child psychiatrist and part-time guidance counselor at the school, and that his initial examination disclosed no apparent abnormalities of personality or behavior patterns. Dr. Fahringer did, however, have several long talks with the Bensons, and as a result Andrew was forbidden to attend motion pictures. The following year, Dr. Fahringer voluntarily offered to examine young Andrew – undoubtedly his interest had been aroused by the amazing dramatic abilities the boy was showing in his extra curricular activities at the school.

Only one such interview ever took place, and it is to be regretted that Dr. Fahringer neither committed his findings to paper nor communicated them to the Bensons before his sudden, shocking death at the hands of an unknown assailant. It is believed (or was believed by the police, at the time) that one of his former patients, committed to an institution as a psychotic, may have been guilty of the crime.

All that we know is that it occurred some short while following a local re-run of the film, *Man in the Attic,* in which Jack Palance essayed the role of Jack the Ripper.

It is interesting, today, to examine some of the so-called 'horror movies' of those years including the re-runs of earlier vehicles starring Boris Karloff, Bela Lugosi, Peter Lorre and a number of other actors.

We cannot say with any certainty, of course, that Andrew Benson was violating the wishes of his foster-parents and secretly attending motion pictures. But if he did, it is quite likely that he would frequent the smaller neighborhood houses, many of which specialized in re-runs. And we do know, from the remarks of fellow classmates during these high school years, that 'Andy' was familiar – almost omnisciently so – with the mannerisms, of these performers.

The evidence is oftentimes conflicting. Joan Charters, for example, is willing to 'swear on a stack of Bibles' that Andrew Benson, at the age of 15, was 'a dead ringer for Peter Lorre – the same bug eyes and everything.' Whereas Nick Dossinger, who attended classes with Benson a year later, insists that he 'looked just like Boris Karloff.'

Granted that adolescence may bring about a considerable increase in height during the period of a year, it is nevertheless difficult to imagine how a 'dead ringer for Peter Lorre' could metamorphize into an asthenic Karloff type.

A mass of testimony is available concerning Andrew Benson during those years, but almost all of it deals with his phenomenal histrionic talent and his startling skill at 'ad lib' impersonations of motion picture actors. Apparently he had given up mimicking his associates and contemporaries almost entirely.

'He said he liked to do actors better, because they were bigger,' says Don Brady, who appeared with him in the senior play. 'I asked him what he meant by "bigger" and he said it was just that – actors were bigger on the screen, sometimes twenty feet tall. He said, "Why bother with little people when you can be big?" Oh, he was a real offbeat character, that one.'

The phrases recur. 'Oddball', and 'screwball', and 'real gone' are picturesque, but hardly enlightening. And there seems to be little recollection of Andrew Benson as a friend or classmate, in the ordinary role of adolescence. It's the imitator who is remembered, with admiration and, frequently, with distaste bordering on actual apprehension.

'He was so good he scared you. But that's when he was doing those impersonations, of course. The rest of the time you scarcely knew he was around.'

'Classes? I guess he did all right. I didn't notice him much.'

'Andrew was a fair student. He could recite when called upon, but he never volunteered. His marks were average. I got the impression he was rather withdrawn.'

'No, he never dated much. Come to think of it, I don't think he went out with girls at all. I never paid much attention to him, except when he was on stage, of course.'

'I wasn't really what you call close to Andy. I don't know anybody who seemed to be friends with him. He was so quiet, outside of the dramatics. And when he got up there, it was like he was a different person – he was real great, you know? We all figured he'd end up at the Pasadena Playhouse.'

The reminiscences of his contemporaries are frequently apt to touch upon matters which did not directly involve Andrew Benson. The years 1956 and 1957 are still remembered, by high school students of the area in particular, as the years of the curfew. It was a voluntary curfew, of course, but it was nevertheless strictly observed by most of the female students during the period of the 'werewolf murders' – that series of savage, still-unsolved crimes which terrorized the community for well over a year. Certain cannibalistic aspects of the slaying of the five young women led to the 'werewolf' appellation on the part of the sensation-mongering press. The *Wolf Man* series made by Universal had been revived, and perhaps this had something to do with the association.

But to return to Andrew Benson; he grew up, went to school, and lived the normal life of a dutiful stepson. If his foster-parents were a bit strict, he made no complaints. If they punished him because they suspected he sometimes slipped out of his room at night, he made no complaint or denials. If they seemed apprehensive lest he be disobeying their set injunctions not to attend the movies, he offered no overt defiance.

The only known clash between Andrew Benson and his family came about as a result of their flat refusal to allow a television set in their home. Whether or not they were concerned about the possible encouragement of Andrew's mimicry or whether they had merely developed an allergy to Lawrence Welk and his ilk is difficult to determine. Nevertheless, they balked at the acquisition of a TV set. Andrew begged and pleaded, pointed out that he 'needed' television as an aid to a future dramatic career. His argument had some justification, for in his senior year, Andrew had indeed been 'scouted' by the famous Pasadena Playhouse, and there was even some talk of a future professional career without the necessity of formal training.

But the Bensons were adamant on the television question; as

far as we can determine, they remained adamant right up to the day of their death.

The unfortunate circumstances occurred at Balboa, where the Bensons owned a small cottage and maintained a little cabin-cruiser. The elder Bensons and Andrew were heading for Catalina Channel when the cruiser overturned in choppy waters. Andrew managed to cling to the craft until rescued, but his foster-parents were gone. It was a common enough accident; you've probably seen something just like it in the movies a dozen times.

Andrew, just turned 18, was left an orphan once more – but an orphan in full possession of a lovely home, and with the expectation of coming into a sizeable inheritance when he reached twenty-one. The Benson estate was administered by the family attorney, Justin L. Fowler, and he placed young Andrew on an allowance of forty dollars a week – an amount sufficient for a recent graduate of high school to survive on, but hardly enough to maintain him in luxury.

It is to be feared that violent scenes were precipitated between the young man and his attorney. There is no point in recapitulating them here, or in condemning Fowler for what may seem – on the surface of it – to be the development of a fixation.

But up until the night that he was struck down by a hit-and-run driver in the street before his house, Attorney Fowler seemed almost obsessed with the desire to prove that the Benson lad was legally incompetent, or worse. Indeed, it was his investigation which led to the uncovering of what few facts are presently available concerning the life of Andrew Benson.

Certain other hypotheses – one hesitates to dignify them with the term 'conclusions' – he apparently extrapolated from these meager findings, or fabricated them out of thin air. Unless, of course, he did manage to discover details which he never actually disclosed. Without the support of such details there is no way of authenticating what seem to be a series of fantastic conjectures.

A random sampling, as remembered from various conversations Fowler had with the authorities, will suffice.

'I don't think the kid is even human, for that matter. Just because he showed up on those orphanage steps, you call him a foundling. Changeling might be a better word for it. Yes, I know they don't believe in such things any more. And if you talk about life-forms from other planets, they laugh at you and tell you to join the Fortean Society. So happens, I'm a member.

'Changeling? It's probably a more accurate term than the narrow meaning implies. I'm talking about the way he changes when he sees these movies. No, don't take my word for it – ask anyone who's ever seen him act. Better still, ask those who never saw him on a stage, but just watched him imitate movie performers in private. You'll find out he did a lot more than just imitate. He *becomes* the actor. Yes, I mean he undergoes an actual physical transformation. Chameleon. Or some other form of life. Who can say?

'No, I don't pretend to understand it. I know it's not "scientific" according to the way you define science. But that doesn't mean it's impossible. There are a lot of life-forms in the universe, and we can only guess at some of them. Why shouldn't there be one that's abnormally sensitive to mimicry?

'You know what effect the movies can have on so-called "normal" human beings, under certain conditions. It's a hypnotic state, this movie-viewing, and you can ask the psychologists for confirmation. Darkness, concentration, suggestion – all the elements are present. And there's post-hypnotic suggestion, too. Again, psychiatrists will back me up on that. Most people tend to identify with various characters on the screen. That's where our hero worship comes in, that's why we have western-movie fans, and detective fans, and all the rest. Supposedly ordinary people come out of the theater and fantasy themselves as the heroes and heroines they saw up there on the screen; imitate them, too.

'That's what Andrew Benson did, of course. Only suppose he could carry it one step further? Suppose he was capable of *being* what he saw portrayed? And he chose to *be* the villains? I tell you, it's time to investigate those killings of a few years back, all of them. Not just the murder of those girls, but the murder of the two doctors who examined Benson when he was a child, and the death of his foster-parents, too. I don't think any of these things were accidents. I think some people got too close to the secret, and Benson put them out of the way.

'Why? How should I know why? Any more than I know what he's looking for when he watches the movies. But he's looking for something, I can guarantee that. Who knows what purpose such a life-form can have, or what he intends to do with his power? All I can do is warn you.'

It is easy to dismiss Attorney Fowler as a paranoid type, though perhaps unfair, in that we cannot evaluate the reasons for his outburst. That he knew (or believed he knew) something is self-evident. As a matter of fact, on the very evening of his death he was apparently about to put his findings on paper.

Deplorably, all that he ever set down was a preamble, in the form of a quotation from Eric Voegelin, concerning rigid pragmatic attitudes of 'scientism', so-called:

ᶠ(1) the assumption that the mathematized science of natural phenomena is a model science to which all other sciences ought to conform; (2) that all realms of being are accessible to the methods of the sciences of phenomena; and (3) that all reality which is not accessible to sciences of phenomena is either irrelevant or, in the more radical form of the dogma, illusionary.'

But Attorney Fowler is dead, and we deal with the living; with Max Schick, for example, the motion-picture and television agent who visited Andrew Benson at his home shortly after the death of the elder Bensons, and offered him an immediate contract.

'You're a natural,' Schick declared. 'Never mind with the Pasadena Playhouse bit. I can spot you right now, believe me! With what you got, we'll back Brando right off the map! Of course, we gotta start small, but I know just the gimmick. Main thing is to establish you in a starring slot right away. None of this stock-contract jazz, get me? The studios aren't handing 'em out any more in the first place, and even if you landed one, you'd end up on Cloud Nowhere. No, the deal is to get you a lead and billing right off the bat. And like I said, I got the angle.

'We go to a small independent producer, get it? Must be a dozen of 'em operating right now, and all of 'em making the same thing. Only one kind of picture that combines low budgets with big grosses, and that's a science fiction movie.

'Yeah, you heard me, a science fiction movie. Whaddya mean, you never saw one? Are you kidding? How about that? You mean you never saw any science fiction pictures at all?

'Oh, your folks, eh? Had to sneak out? And they only show that kind of stuff at the downtown houses?

'Well look, kid, it's about time, that's all I can say. It's about time! Hey, just so's you know what we're talking about, you better get on the ball and take in one right away. Sure, I'm positive, there must be one playing a downtown first run now. Why don't you go this afternoon? I got some work to finish up here at the office – run you down in my car and you can go on to the show, meet me back there when you get out.

'Sure, you can take the car after you drop me off. Be my guest.'

So Andrew Benson saw his first science fiction movie. He drove there and back in Max Schick's car (coincidentally enough, it was the late afternoon of the day when Attorney Fowler became a hit-and-run victim) and Schick has good reason to remember Andrew Benson's reappearance at his office just after dusk.

'He had a look on his face that was out of this world,' Schick says.

' "How'd you like the picture?" I ask him.

' "It was wonderful," he tells me. "Just what I've been looking for all these years. And to think I didn't know."

' "Didn't know what?" I ask. But he isn't talking to me any more. You can see that. He's talking to himself.

' "I thought there must be something like that," he says. "Something better than Dracula, or Frankenstein's Monsters, or all the rest. Something bigger, more powerful. Something I could really be. And now I know. And now I'm going to." '

Max Schick is unable to maintain coherency from this point on. But his direct account is not necessary. We are, unfortunately, all too well aware of what happened next.

Max Schick sat there in his chair and watched Andrew Benson *change*.

He watched him *grow*. He watched him put forth the eyes, the stalks, the writhing tentacles. He watched him twist and tower, filling the room and then *overflowing* until the flimsy stucco walls collapsed and there was nothing but the green, gigantic horror, the sixty-foot-high monstrosity that may have been born in a screenwriter's brain or may have been spawned beyond the stars, but certainly existed and drew nourishment from realms far from a three-dimensional world or three-dimensional concepts of sanity.

Max Schick will never forget that night and neither, of course, will anybody else.

That was the night the monster destroyed Los Angeles . . .

THE PROFESSOR PLAYS IT SQUARE

BUGSY and me are sitting in the lobby of the Cash Inn when this character crawls out of the woodwork.

'Look,' Bugsy says. 'A cucumber!'

Sure enough, this is a real green specimen – a little old shriveled-up guy with white hair and rimless cheaters. He is carrying an umbrella and wearing a black suit which he probably bought special for President McKinley's funeral.

'Dig the umbrella,' Bugsy whispers. 'What do you suppose he's lugging that around for?'

'Maybe he thinks the roof leaks,' I tell him.

But I have to admit the old party is kind of conspicuous, because the Cash Inn caters to what you might call an exclusive-type clientele. Meaning normal citizens like Bugsy and me, who don't go in for whacky outfits. For instance, this evening Bugsy is dressed for dinner in an ordinary black-and-white checked suit with matching spats, and I am sort of casual in orange trousers and a green shirt to match the beret.

Most of the other guests in this pad wear pretty much the same kind of duds, so we are a little surprised when this old geezer wanders up to us and makes with the mouth.

'I beg your pardon,' he says, 'but would you two gentlemen happen to be gamblers, by any chance?'

'Not by chance – on purpose,' says Bugsy. 'What's with you, Dad?'

'Permit me to introduce myself,' the old character mumbles. 'I am Professor Ladislaus Glockenspiel, of Parnell University.'

Bugsy gets up and does the honors. 'Lay five on me, Pops,' he

56

tells him. 'I am Bugsy Roach from Pasadena, and this here is my business associate, Mr. Knuckle-Nose Mahoney.'

'A pleasure,' the Professor says, flipping me some skin. 'And where are you from, Mr. Mahoney?'

'A small island just off San Francisco,' I inform him. 'I forget the name.'

'But you gentlemen are gamblers, I hope,' he murmurs. 'They told me this was a sporting rendezvous.'

'The best in the West,' I say. 'Bugsy and me, we always hole up here when we hit town, on account of the homey atmosphere. For instance, if you're down on your luck, you can always match the desk clerk double or nothing for your room. And see that weighing machine over in the corner of the lobby? If you guess your weight right, it pays off a jackpot in pennies.'

'All the comforts of home,' Bugsy chimes in. 'When a guy suffers from insomnia, like I do, it is a great comfort to have a nice big slot-machine right there in your room, so you can get up and try your luck to pass the time away. Also, it is the only hotel I know that prints the daily race results on the menus.'

'How fascinating!' says the Professor. 'You simply must tell me more. And I hope I might have the pleasure of learning about games of chance from you through actual experience.'

'You mean you'd like to play with us?' Bugsy asks. 'You're looking for some action?'

'Precisely,' the Professor answers. 'Looking for action – what a picturesque phrase! How idiomatic!'

'Please,' I say. 'No insults.'

'I beg your pardon,' the Professor mutters. 'I am merely interested in everything pertaining to gambling. The laws of chance have always absorbed me, and I came out here for the express purpose of studying them. I've saved my money for years just to make this trip.'

'How much lettuce you got in the patch?' Bugsy wants to know.

The Professor frowns and looks blank.

'He means cabbage,' I explain. 'Moola. Loot. You got the scratch?'

'I *am* wearing my winter underwear, gentlemen,' the Professor admits. 'But—'

'Dough,' I tell him. 'You loaded?'

'Oh!' He puts a grin on his chin. 'Well, I don't exactly have a fortune in my possession. But I thought that with eleven thousand dollars, perhaps I could learn a little something.' And he hauls a roll out of his vest pocket.

I look at Bugsy and Bugsy looks at me. Then we both look at the roll. The manager of the Cash Inn passes by and gives us a dirty look, because I guess he does not like to see us drool all over his nice new carpet.

'Professor, you have a real deal,' Bugsy tells him. 'For eleven grand I think we can promise you that you'll learn a whole lot. And you sure come to the right teachers.'

'Wonderful!' the Professor says. 'I was hoping I might start tonight, if you're not too busy—'

'Well, we did have a date with a stiff who runs a prayer meeting,' I admit. 'But he'd probably try to rip the bricks on us, anyway.'

'You were going to church?' the Professor asks.

'No,' Bugsy explains. 'A prayer meeting is a private crap game. A stiff is a guy who's down on his luck. And to rip the bricks means to switch the dice.'

'Cheating?' The Professor shakes his head. 'I wouldn't want to have anything to do with dishonest players.'

'Then stick with us,' I tell him. 'We'll get up a nice friendly little game of stud poker.' I turn to Bugsy. 'Let's use your room,' I suggest. 'How about inviting Nifty Novotny, and Cold-deck Charlie and old Sticky-fingers?'

'Sorry,' Bugsy answers. 'Nifty Novotny is still hiding out after that job he pulled in Las Vegas. Cold-deck Charlie is doing five in San Quentin, according to what I hear around town. And old Sticky-fingers has a regular night job, remember? He's peddling reefers down at the drive-in restaurant.'

'Well, don't worry,' I say to the Professor. 'I'm sure we can find some other good friends of ours who are just as trustworthy. I'll get on the phone and you go on up to Bugsy's room and get started with your education.'

Well, the way it turns out, I have no trouble lining up three finks for the game. I choose some small-time operators on purpose, because there is no sense complicating the details by cutting them in. The Professor is our pupil, and we are going to do all the teaching, so we might as well collect the tuition fee.

When the game gets started, we commence learning him things right off. For example, he finds out that a deck of cards is called a devil, and that he is supposed to sit between Bugsy and me when he plays. This is called a cucumber sandwich, but we do not tell him that. We figure there is plenty for him to learn as it is, without bothering his head with such useless information. And believe me, when anybody sits down to play poker between Bugsy and me, such information *is* useless.

I must say this for Professor Glockenspiel, though – he is an eager student and he does not seem to worry about paying for his lessons.

Right off the bat he spends two hundred bucks to find out that the pair of kings he holds is called a pair of bulls – but does not beat my three fives.

Then he shells out another hunk of dough to discover that aces are called bullets or dreadnaughts, but do not beat the straight Bugsy has in his hand.

After that we take six hundred clams to demonstrate that aces and eights are the Dead Man's Hand, and a grand or so to prove that twos are called deuces, and cannot beat a full house. We also teach him never to draw to an inside straight, and finally we demonstrate that four of a kind is better than a flush.

By the time night-school is over, the Professor is out his eleven grand, but we hope he has the satisfaction of being a finished student.

The funny part is, he does seem to be satisfied. When he gets up to leave he is still smiling. 'Thank you for a very rewarding experience, gentlemen,' he says. 'It is kind of you to put up with an amateur like myself.'

'The pleasure is ours,' Bugsy assures him. 'Too bad you don't have better luck.'

'On the contrary, it is a rewarding experience,' the Professor says. 'I have learned far more than I hoped.'

'If you want to try your luck again, be sure to look us up,' Bugsy tells him, as he eases him out the door.

But Professor Glockenspiel shakes his head and sort of sighs. 'I doubt if I shall have the opportunity,' he says. 'My losses tonight represent the savings of twenty years.'

'What if you won?' I want to know.

'Odd that you should ask me,' he answers. 'I was hoping to increase my capital to endow Parnell University with a special chair.'

'You can buy a mighty fancy chair for eleven grand,' Bugsy says. 'Maybe even gold-plated.'

'I am referring to a chair of research,' the Professor tells him. 'The University refuses to allow me funds to pursue my hobby, so I thought I might win enough to institute a teaching department of my own. But apparently fortune is not with me.'

'Tough,' I say. 'But if you do get hold of any more geedus, we'll be around. Always glad to show you a little action.'

Then we say good night, and Bugsy and I salute the loot.

'A big score,' he grins. 'The kind you hit once in a lifetime. Why the mark does not even give us any grief with a beef. Too bad he is cleaned out.'

'Let's stick around a few days,' I suggest. 'Maybe he will wire home for money.'

'What can we lose?' Bugsy agrees. So we stay over at the Cash Inn, and for the next couple of afternoons we go out to the track to play the bangtails and for the next few nights we watch the wheels go around at the tables.

And sure enough, on the third evening the Professor shows up in the lobby again. He has a friend with him – a tall, skinny kid with a crewcut like a worn-out welcome mat. Regular Joe College type, horn-rimmed glasses and all.

The Professor comes right over and lays on the introduction. 'This is Oswald Fing,' he says. 'One of my star pupils from Parnell University. He is out here on vacation, and I told him how royally you gentlemen entertained me the other evening. He is anxious for a little session.'

Bugsy and I stare at the square, and then Bugsy gets the Professor over in a corner. 'You know how luck is,' he whispers. 'Can he afford to lose?'

The Professor winks at him. 'The young man is, as you say, loaded. And I was wondering, if I brought him to you gentlemen for a game, if I might venture to claim a share of the – er – profits. I shall not be participating in the session myself, you understand. I am merely – what is the term? – a steerer.'

Bugsy shakes his head. 'Naughty, naughty!' he says. 'But I see you learn fast. And I think we can cut you in. Shall we say one-third?'

'Fair enough,' the Professor agrees. 'Now, can you find a few other players for the evening? I would suggest you select some rather substantial investors.'

Bugsy tips me off and I round up Big Mike Rafferty and Philadelphia Phil, two of the largest operators in these parts. There is no sense telling them what is going to happen – it is going to be a little secret between Bugsy, the Professor and me.

This time we play in my room, which has the advantage of being soundproof. Something tells me this kid Oswald Fing may not be as good a loser as the Professor, and I do not wish to disturb the neighbors with his cries of anguish when we lay it on him.

Right away we explain to him that this game calls for a bit of action, as Big Mike Rafferty and Philadelphia Phil do not indulge for peanuts, and Bugsy and me have eleven grand to work with, plus another four of our own to feed to the kitty.

Oswald Fing looks at the Professor and shakes his head. 'You did not tell me the stakes are so high,' he says. 'And I know absolutely nothing about poker.'

'Don't worry about a thing,' the Professor answers. 'I can assure you, you'll learn in a hurry with these able instructors.' Then he smiles at Oswald Fing and winks at me, and the game starts.

That is the last smile anybody sees around the table from then on. Because something funny happens to the game.

Oh, Oswald Fing doesn't know anything about poker – that is easy enough to see from the start. He cannot even call his hands, but merely lays them down and lets the Professor do the talking.

The trouble is, he lays down nothing but winning hands.

Instead of sticking in every pot, the way the Professor does the other night, he drops out half the time. But whenever he does stay, he has the cards.

If I draw three tens, he sticks on three jacks. If Bugsy holds a straight, Oswald has a flush. If Big Mike Rafferty or Philadelphia Phil catch full houses, there is Oswald with four of a kind.

Either he has a sure thing or he folds. Not once does he call without the top hand, and not once does he bluff. Rafferty and Phil find that out the hard way, and I figure they blow about twenty grand before they have enough. Then they get up and leave.

This suits me fine, because I know now that something is very much haywire, and I tip Bugsy the nod. This means we get down to business with a new deck. This new deck happens to be one of Bugsy's specials.

We bring it into play, and all at once the kid jumps up.

'Not that deck!' he says.

'What do you mean?' I ask. 'Are you insinuating that we'd cheat?'

'Yes, dear boy,' the Professor chimes in. 'Don't you trust these gentlemen?'

'Call it a hunch,' Oswald says. 'I want the other deck.'

So there is nothing to do but bring back the old deck and

hope for the best. I look at Bugsy's pile and my own and figure we have maybe six grand left between us – from all the dough we won the other night plus our own. We will have to sweat it out.

And the next hand that comes up brings out the old perspiration in a hurry. I find myself sitting with aces back to back. As the cards go around, I cop a third bullet. I bet it up and Bugsy drops. Oswald stays, showing a straight in the works.

On the seventh card I catch the fourth ace. That's when I shoot the works.

Oswald sees me – and raises.

I give Bugsy a peek at my hand and he grunts. Then he shoves the rest of his chips over to me. I call.

And Oswald lays down his straight. Only it is a straight flush, king high.

I am busted.

Also, I am pretty angry. In fact, I am just about to get up and reach for a heater which I happen to have laying around in the top drawer under my socks, when the Professor stops me.

'Sit down,' he says. 'I think I have what you're looking for.'

Sure enough, he holds a big equalizer in his hand, but he is not giving it to me – merely pointing.

'Hey, what's the big idea?' Bugsy wants to know.

'You sit down, too,' the Professor suggests. 'I believe I am holding what you call a Harlem hand.' He grins. 'You see, I have done a bit of studying on my own, gentlemen.'

We sit there and watch while Oswald Fing counts up his winnings.

'Forty thousand dollars,' he announces. 'You were right, Professor.'

'Of course I was,' the Professor tells him. 'I have the utmost confidence in my hunches. And in yours.'

'You can't cheat us—' Bugsy snarls.

'This isn't cheating,' the Professor says. 'So let us have no more of that kind of talk. And I suggest you gentlemen remain seated until after we have left, or else I shall be forced to ventilate your ventricles.'

I do not understand this jive, but the gun tells me all I wish to know. So I sit there until they walk out, and Bugsy keeps me company.

Afterwards we are too weak to get up. Besides, being broke, there is no place for us to go.

I guess the Professor and his pupil check out the same night. Anyway, the next day they are gone. Bugsy and I stick around, hoping we can raise the dough to pay our hotel bill.

We are still there a week later, and we are still arguing about what happens. We can't figure out why Oswald wins that way.

Not until one afternoon when Big Mike Rafferty comes up to us with a New York paper in his hand.

'Here,' he says. 'Read about your friends.'

I sneak a peek at a little item on page 5. It tells me all I want to know:

PROFESSOR ENDOWS UNIVERSITY CHAIR

Professor Ladislaus Glockenspiel has just endowed Parnell University with a $40,000 Chair of Parapsychology. He will use the money to continue his research in ESP, or extra-sensory perception.

Readers may recall his experiments with student subjects; among them, Oswald Fing, who amazes experts by running through a pack of ordinary playing cards and calling them off correctly 52 times out of 52.

When questioned as to the source of his funds, Professor Glockenspiel said he had recently received contributions from philanthropists in the West.

That's what the article says, and I don't pretend I understand it all. I don't dig this 'Parapsychology' or this 'extra-sensory perception' bit, either.

Only one thing I'm sure of – 'philanthropists'. That's just another word for a couple of suckers.

Meaning Bugsy and me.

BLOCK THAT METAPHOR

It was a formal affair – white shorts and tails – and Lane Borden wondered just how well Vorm would fit in.

The servants and attachés here at the Embassy were used to extra-terrestials, but even they seemed disturbed by Vorm.

If he had been a mere robot, now, there wouldn't be any problem, but the idea of a living intelligent brain in a synthetic body was difficult to accept. The body itself was metallic and humanoid in its general contours. But there were some differences.

An engineer would probably grant the advantages of six visual perceptors, or 'eyes' situated equidistantly around the entire cranial compartment, but the knowledge that Vorm really had 'eyes in the back of his head' and could observe everything in a room simultaneously had its unnerving effect on others. Vorm's 'mouth' was just a speaking-tube, and as for his 'nose'—

Lane Borden remembered what had happened earlier in the afternoon, when he'd conducted Vorm into his own apartments at the Embassy for a little informal chat. That's when Borden's fiancée had made an unexpected appearance.

Borden was proud of Margaret Zurich. She was a strikingly beautiful woman and a intergalactically famous pianist – one of the few who still excelled in the ancient art of nonelectronic musicianship.

She seemed startled by Vorm's appearance, and even more startled when he acknowledged her introduction by abruptly reaching up, unscrewing the flaring spout above his speaking-tube, and inserting a blunt nozzle in its place. This he took from the large diplomatic pouch strapped to his waist, dipping into it casually, as a matter of course.

Margaret Zurich pretended not to notice, but Borden could tell that she was disconcerted. Borden knew that later he must take her aside and explain that nose-changing was a token of polite greeting in Vorm's world. Vorm's race did not need noses, per se. In the completely prostheticized body, the nose was now only a tool. The diplomatic pouch Vorm carried must carry a dozen different nasal attachments, each one designed for practical use. Borden knew of one that served as a drill, another which was a sort of acetylene torch, still another which was merely a great razor-sharp cutting instrument. These were all useful to Vorm's race in the mines of their native planet.

Yes, Borden would do his best to make Margaret understand, but it wouldn't be easy. He'd have to try and convey some hint of Vorm's alien thought processes; give an intimation of what it must be like to have super-vision and super-hearing, too. Vorm never slept, he was not chained to the physiological demands of eating and voiding, he was never subject to physical ailments or deterioration. Margaret would just have to accept his alien qualities. She was a cultured and intelligent person, not like the mobs out in the street who went around yelling, 'Down with the dirty Mechs.' That's what they called Vorm's race – Mechs. Mechanical people. It was all political propaganda, of course. The opposition party had mining interests on other planets – they didn't like to see the government trading or doing business with Vorm's race. So they spread their scare-reports about mechanical monsters, played on religious prejudice ('Mechs have no souls') and planted rumors that Mechs had no regard for human rights or human lives.

Borden would set Margaret straight, and yet he had to admit that Vorm wasn't easy to understand. He seemed to have no empathy for people. And he took everything quite literally.

For example, before Margaret left the room, she and Borden embraced. Vorm didn't comprehend the meaning of the gesture; he asked Borden about it later. It wasn't that he meant to be rude. He was merely voicing an honest curiosity.

Borden tried to tell him something about physical contact, and sexual relationship as well, but the whole concept of functioning flesh was strange to the prosthetic being.

'You mean to say your race exists without any notion of love?' Borden mused. 'I must confess that surprises me. I just can't seem to get it through my head.'

Vorm reached into the diplomatic pouch and pulled out a gleaming nasal attachment. 'I could drill it in,' he suggested.

Borden managed to restrain his amusement. 'You don't understand,' he said. 'I was merely using a figure of speech. Yours is a realistic race.'

'Very,' Vorm acknowledged. 'Perhaps that is why we don't comprehend your emotions.'

'But you do have feelings of your own. You know what I mean when I speak of fear, greed, pride. And you have a keen aesthetic appreciation. Take music, for example—'

'Ah, yes,' Vorm replied, in amplified excitement. 'You promised to play something for me when you brought me in here, did you not?'

'Gladly,' Borden told him. And he was glad of the reminder. It would be easier to play than to continue the discussion on an abstract plane. Besides, the music might help drown out the disconcerting murmur which was faintly audible from outside the Embassy. All day long the crowds had been parading up and down, back and forth, carrying their stupid banners. DON'T MIX WITH MECHS! and NO TRADE WITH THE ZOMBIES! were the mildest inscriptions dreamed up by the Opposition. And the foolish mob kept shouting, 'We know you've got a Mech in there! Will you bring him out or do you want us to come in and get him?'

Well, they wouldn't come in. Borden had the gates locked and guards posted. Still, it was embarrassing under the circumstances. He couldn't very well go out there and explain that the government needed to maintain cordial diplomatic relations with Vorm's race, and that it was important that he entertain this Mech visitor. He couldn't make them believe that the sinister rumors about mechanical monsters being murderers were falsely planted for political reasons. The mob hated Mechs and that was that.

But music hath charms, and Borden knew how to play the role of a charmer. He had a collection of antique tapes, and he put on a few for his visitor. Vorm seemed to enjoy mild dissonances – the finale of Prokofiev's *Chout*, the rhythms of Villa-Lobos' *Urapuri*, Respighi's *Feste Roman*, and other primitive examples of older 'symphonic' musical compositions.

Seeing that he was absorbed with the entertainment, Borden excused himself and went to dress, leaving his guest happily twiddling with his stereophonic and binaural ear-vents.

Vorm's preoccupation continued long enough for Borden to get down into the dining hall and check on dinner arrangements; long enough for him to admit and greet the guests who arrived – awkwardly, but sensibly – through a rear entrance. It just wasn't safe to use the front entry, with the mob outside. As it grew darker, the crowd increased; Opposition agitators had showed up. They were going to make a big demonstration, Borden knew, but there was no help for it.

He was just thankful that most of those whom he had invited for dinner actually showed up, despite the unpleasant situation. Government people, for the most part, they knew it was necessary to treat Vorm with hospitality. If Vorm returned to his own planet with a favorable account of his visit, a commercial treaty might be concluded. That was vital.

So Borden welcomed his guests, and then he conducted Vorm into the hall and introduced him around. For the most part, the humans managed to conceal whatever strain or agitation his presence inspired, but there was a noticeable increase in the consumption of before-dinner cocktails. Lawrence, the butler (it was a part of Embassy tradition to employ actual human beings as servants) circulated with his tray for a good half-hour or more before dinner was announced.

Vorm went in with Margaret Zurich on his arm. She displayed admirable composure. Again, Borden was proud of her, and he had no reason to be ashamed of his guests. They ate and drank quite naturally, and pretended not to notice that Vorm merely sat there and employed his oral orifice for speaking purposes only. If he felt awkward – or experienced actual repugnance – at the spectacle of human beings ingesting nourishment, he did not betray his reaction. His speaking-tube was in constant use throughout the long meal, and he seemed pleased to meet many officials and dignitaries.

Borden noticed that he had inserted a different nasal attachment in honor of the occasion. It was a star-shaped instrument, obviously ornamental, for it was studded with diamonds. Several of the ladies openly admired it. Borden wondered what they would have said if Vorm had chosen instead to wear his drill or perhaps the long, razor-like knife. Surely the ladies would have remembered the 'murdering monster' stories and reacted unpleasantly.

But there were no untoward incidents during the course of the dinner, and Borden was quite relieved at its successful conclusion. He led his guests into the drawing room and announced that Margaret would play a few selections in honor of their distinguished visitor.

Some of the guests had never actually seen an old-fashioned 'piano' before, but all of them were aware of Margaret's reputation as an artist. They settled down quite happily to enjoy the impromptu musicale.

Borden and Vorm sat together, directly before the instrument. Oddly enough, Vorm seemed to be familiar with the mechanism of the 'piano'. But then, music fascinated his race.

Margaret's repertoire was classical. She specialized, of course, in the three Bs – Bartok, Brubeck, and Bernstein – and Borden sat back, beaming in pride at her performance.

'Do you play?' Vorm asked, softly.

'A very little,' Borden admitted. 'But I lack the touch. I wish I had her fingers. Or a tenth of her talent. Sometimes I think I wasn't cut out for diplomacy. I should have been a—'

Borden jumped. Everyone started at the tinkling sound, then stared at the pavement block on the tesselated floor. Through the broken window came the clamor of the mob outside.

Lawrence hurried in and whispered to Borden. He rose.

'Please, don't be alarmed,' he said. 'There has been a slight accident downstairs. I'll attend to it. Margaret, if you'll be good enough to continue—'

And she *did* continue, while Borden raced down the hall, then took the steps two at a time. Lawrence followed him with a force-gun such as the guards were holding in the foyer below.

'Nasty,' the butler murmured. 'They got through the gates, somehow. It's all the men can do to keep them from breaking down the door. Captain Rollins is afraid they'll have to open fire soon unless something is done to disperse them. He wants your orders—'

Borden nodded and brushed past him.

'Wait, sir!' Lawrence quavered. 'You aren't going out there, are you? Here, you forgot the gun—'

Borden nodded again, but kept going. At the door, Captain Rollins stepped up to intercept him. Borden walked past him and opened the door.

The roar of the crowd struck him like a great blow.

'Give us the Mech! We know he's in there!'

Borden raised his hands, palms outward, to show he was unarmed. The gesture had its inevitable, immemorial quieting effect.

Slowly, he began to speak.

Afterwards he couldn't quite remember just what it was he had to say. But words come easily to the trained diplomat, and Borden had risen to his present position due to superior qualifications.

He started out by telling the mob they had nothing to fear.

Yes, there was a Mech inside, but couldn't they see that guards had been posted all around the building? The Mech couldn't possibly escape to harm anyone. Besides, he didn't want to do any harm. Right now he was listening to music. The Mech was a music lover! And if they didn't believe it, they could hear for themselves, through the window.

So there was absolutely no danger. The government had seen to that. The Mech was guarded, would be guarded until tomorrow when he'd return to his own planet. He had come here under government invitation, to conclude a treaty. The government needed the Mechs to mine metals for the galaxy. There was no cause for alarm. The guards would remain here all night and tomorrow they'd escort the Mech to the launch-ing-site. In fact, the Mech thought the guards were here to protect *him* – he was afraid of people! Wasn't that something? The Mech was actually afraid of this crowd! If it hadn't been for the music, he'd probably be hiding under his bed right now!

That got a laugh from the mob, and after that the rest was simple. In five minutes Borden managed to break up the assemblage. In ten minutes the street in front of the Embassy was almost cleared. In fifteen minutes he was able to turn matters over to Captain Rollins and rejoin his guests.

It rather startled Borden to find Vorm waiting for him at the foot of the stairs.

'I am sorry, but I had to come,' Vorm said. 'When I knew there was trouble, I realized the cause.'

'It was all a mistake,' Borden told him. 'A misunder-standing.'

'Gracious of you to say so,' Vorm answered, his cranium bobbing. 'But I heard what happened. They meant to destroy me, and you turned them away. You saved me.'

'Do not be offended. They just don't understand.'

'I am not offended. It is just that I wanted you to know that I admire your bravery. You see, I do possess certain of your emotions after all. While our race does not comprehend love, it

71

knows admiration. And it knows gratitude. I am grateful to you, Mr. Borden. I must reward you.'

'Nonsense! I want no reward. I'm well-satisfied with what I have.'

'I will think of something suitable.'

'Forget it, please.'

'I never forget anything.'

'Shall we join the others?'

They did, and the episode concluded. Margaret made no attempt to continue playing; in a short while the guests made their departure. Although reasonably sure that there was no longer any danger from the crowd, Borden insisted that they again use the rear exit. As for Margaret, he persuaded her to stay over for the night. 'I'll feel safer if you do,' he told her.

'Very well, if you insist.'

She said good night to Vorm and Lawrence took her down the hall to one of the guest rooms at the end of the corridor.

Borden was left alone with Vorm, but not for long. He felt positively embarrassed by Vorm's constant protestations of gratitude. 'I must show my appreciation, somehow,' Vorm kept saying.

'Please, it isn't necessary.'

'But isn't there something you want—'

'Not a thing.' Borden shook his head emphatically. 'Now, if I can be excused—'

'That is right. You must rest, is it not so? There is so much I do not understand about humans.'

'Good night.'

'Good night.'

Borden retired.

He slept fitfully, disturbed by dreams. As a result he did not fall into deep slumber until dawn, and he must have overslept as a consequence, because when he awoke Lawrence was shaking him and mumbling something to the effect that Vorm was gone.

'Gone?' Borden sat upright in bed. 'But I was to take him to the launching-site this morning.'

'Captain Rollins did so, sir. And knowing you were tired—'

'But I meant to say good-by.'

'It really wasn't necessary. Vorm told me to express his thanks for all your kindnesses and to assure you of his gratitude—'

'That, again!'

Lawrence smiled. 'I'm afraid so, sir. You seem to have made quite an impression on him because of your conduct last night. A diplomatic triumph, if I may say so.' He coughed. 'Vorm told me to give you this,' he said.

'What is it?'

'A farewell gift, I believe.'

Lawrence extended the small white box and Borden fumbled with the wrappings.

'What on earth for? More gratitude, I presume?'

'Exactly.' Lawrence smiled. 'He said he'd spent hours trying to think of something for a man who claimed he had everything. Fortunately, he told me, he forgets nothing. And he happened to remember that you had expressed a certain wish last night, which he was happy to be able to fulfill.'

'A wish? I don't recall—'

'He said that now you would be able to play the piano.'

Borden put down the package very slowly.

He stood up, thinking about Vorm. Vorm, who didn't understand love, but who knew gratitude. Vorm, who didn't comprehend human flesh and its frailty, but who knew that he could change parts of his body at will, simply unscrewing one instrument and putting in another. Vorm, who took everything quite literally. Vorm, who could install a nasal appendage which was like a great razor. Vorm, who had heard him say, 'I wish I had her fingers.'

'What's the matter, sir?' Lawrence murmured. 'Aren't you even going to look at your gift?'

But Borden was already running down the hall towards Margaret's room.

WHEEL AND DEAL

HARRIGAN arrived at work around nine o'clock. It was a Monday morning and he was dull-eyed and draggy-tailed, but as usual he brightened considerably when he surveyed his kingdom.

The big showroom was immaculate, and the huge lot next door looked imposing, with its row of used models. But best of all he liked the signs and banners which proclaimed his rule over the domain.

HAPPY HARRIGAN
King of the Auto-Erotics
NEW AND USED FEMALES – ALL MAKES
'WE'RE TRADING WILD!'

Harrigan squared his shoulders proudly and marched into his private office. There was a young punk sitting there, and for a minute Harrigan gave him his customer-smile, until he remembered who the fellow was. Phil Thompson, that was his name; Harrigan had hired him on Saturday as a new salesman.

'Ready to hit the ball, eh?' he said. 'That's good. Suppose the first thing I ought to do is show you around the place.'

The punk stood up. 'Gee, that'd be great, Mr. Harrigan.'

'Call me Happy – everybody does,' Harrigan told him, deftly popping an ulcerizor into his mouth. 'Most important thing to remember is that we're all friends here, Phil. This is a friendly business. That's something we tell all our customers. We don't just sell females – we sell service.'

74

Phil nodded and trailed him out of the office and across the showroom.

'Which reminds me,' Harrigan murmured, over his shoulder. 'When I hired you Saturday you said you didn't have much experience with females.'

'I was just thinking of the mechanical end,' Phil explained. 'But like I told you, I've always been crazy about 'em, ever since I was a kid. Used to spend all my time monkeying around with my Dad's—'

Harrigan nodded absently. 'Well, you don't have to worry about that part of it,' he said. 'Take a look back here – we've got six skilled medics always on the job. We service all types of females ourselves.' He led the youngster into the noisy recesses of the big room behind the showroom, where frowning medics and harried grease-monkeys busied themselves with an imposing array of auto-erotics. Some of the models were only partially assembled, and some were undergoing extensive overhauling.

Harrigan gestured at a group clustered around a rack and raised his voice over the clangor which attended their efforts.

'Working on an old 69 model,' he shouted. 'Complete hysterectomy.'

'You're really thorough, aren't you?' Phil commented.

'Have to be. You know our policy. Every female that goes out of here carries a six months' written guarantee.'

Harrigan walked back into the showroom and the young man followed.

Brice, the senior salesman, was working on a customer – a dignified old geezer, all haunch, paunch and jowl. They were inspecting one of the new 75s; a stunning, streamlined brunette with a forward look. 'Let me open her up for you,' Brice was saying. 'Here, just take a peek at her chassis. She's really built for performance. Auto-erotic transmission, just push a button to select your speed, all the attachments including a voice-tape and a built-in heater. This baby is loaded! And take a look at that rear end! She's got the biggest bustle on the market today.'

'Well, I don't know,' the old geezer muttered. 'Could I get the same thing in a blonde?'

'Anything you like. Platinum, redhead, all the two-tone combinations—'

'Maybe I'd better bring my wife in and let her decide,' the customer said. 'She's kind of got her heart set on a convertible.'

'Convertible, eh?' The salesman winked and nudged him. 'We can put an attachment in this baby in no time.'

Harrigan pulled Phil to one side and lowered his voice to a whisper. 'Just wanted you to get a load of the way we sell 'em in here,' he explained. 'But you're a long way from working the floor with new models. I'm gonna start you outside. It takes a special know-how to deal with blue chip customers.'

He grabbed Phil's arm and ushered him out the rear exit. 'Notice how Brice was handling that guy?' he asked. 'Giving him the old pride-of-ownership routine. Never even mentioned the price. With those customers, money doesn't mean a thing. They just buy to show off. You can tell by looking at him that he won't be using his model more'n once a week, if that often. Probably the kind who just sits in the bedroom and turns over the motor.'

Harrigan blinked in the bright sunlight and popped another ulcerizor into his mouth.

'You won't be working in there, like I said, but it's important you get to know something about the kind of customers we deal with. That's the biggest thing in salesmanship – you've got to be able to spot your customer the minute he walks in.

'Now take that character we just saw. He's the conspicuous-consumption type. All he's interested in is having the biggest, newest, flashiest, most expensive female in town. What the hell does he care about how much it costs; probably has a deal worked out where all his females are company-owned. He trades in and gets a new model every year, fast as they come out. And don't think the manufacturers aren't wise to him – that's why they keep putting on more and more fancy paint jobs and bigger and wider bustles. You and I know a big bustle is just a damned nuisance; it doesn't add anything to the performance of a model or the pleasure you get out of her, and neither do those big bumpers up front. But that's what these kind of customers want.'

'Are they all like that?' Phil inquired.

'Well, most of them. Once in a while we get somebody off the street who's just interested in a strip-job, but we don't make any dough off a naked model. We're out to load 'em good in the new showroom, so we discourage those characters. Let 'em go down the street to the Leering Irishman.'

'What about sports models?'

'Floosies? Never touch 'em. We sell one-owner deals only. None of these souped-up specials.' Harrigan chewed his lip. 'But that's a big business, too. The sports model customer is an odd bird. He's got his own way of showing off. He keeps talking about speed and thrills. With him, it's all a matter of a fast start and a lot of noise. Actually, he usually gets less pleasure out of what he buys than the old codgers. But he talks a good game.'

Harrigan prodded the younger man in the chest. 'There's a couple of other types you should learn to recognize, too,' he said. 'The real show-offs. Guys so rich they can't stand owning anything but a foreign model. Real fancy stuff – voice-tapes with accents, yet, and all kinds of special French attachments.' He sighed. 'But the richest ones of all are worse yet. You know what they go in for? Old models, that's what. Whole fleets of 'em! They're queer for anything with a universal shift – not to use, just to look at. They'll pay a fortune for some antique, give her a face-lift, new paint, rub her up for hours on end. I dunno, some psych told me it was sort of a motor-complex.'

He shrugged and dismissed the subject as they strolled over towards the big lot with its glaring banners waving in the wind.

OKAY USED FEMALES
Guaranteed Clean – One-Owner
YOU MUST BE SATISFIED OR IT'S NO DEAL

'Here's where you'll be starting,' Harrigan said. 'Think you can handle it?'

Young Phil glanced nervously around the lot. Almost sixty models were lined up on display, in neat rows, each chained to a post. Some were old, some were almost brand new, but all were bright and shiny: eye-lights sparkling, teeth gleaming, bodies newly painted.

Harrigan ran his hand appreciatively along the flank of a brownette 74. 'Take this baby, for example,' he said. 'A real creampuff. When we get in a number like this, we call it an executive model. That's the thing to tell the customers – she's just like a new one, except that you don't have to break her in. Here.' He reached over and stuck his key into the ignition. 'Why don't you see for yourself how she handles.'

The model began to purr and vibrate.

'No, I couldn't, not out here—'

'Well, take her into one of the testing booths, then. We always give the customer a trial spin.'

Harrigan squinted at Phil. 'Hey, you look kind of pale. What's the matter?'

'Nothing. It's just that—'

'Now wait a minute. I thought you told me you had some mechanical experience.'

'I did. That is, sort of. I mean, you know how kids are—'

'Don't hand me that. I'll bet you never had a model in your life. Probably your old man wouldn't let you play with anything but an Erector set.'

'But he owned—'

'I know what he owned.' Harrigan looked grim. 'He brought a junker, didn't he? Souped it up, restyled her, like one of those hot-rodder jobs. Come clean, kid – you've never operated a real model at all.'

Phil was blushing. 'Guess you're right, Mr. Harrigan,' he admitted. 'My Dad was kind of old-fashioned, you know. When Mom died, he didn't even want to get us a utility model to do the cooking and housework.'

78

'You got a nerve coming around here and bracing me for a job.'

'Well, I just figured—'

'I know what you figured. You thought you could make a fast buck here.' Harrigan gripped his arm roughly. 'Well, you can. Believe me, kid, you can! Only not unless you change your attitude. What the hell, you'd think we were running some kind of illegal racket or something. Wake up, kid – this is the twenty-first century! The auto-erotic industry is the biggest business in the country.

'Let me tell you something else, son. You're just lucky to be alive today and have such an opportunity. You've read your history-tapes. How'd you like to have been born a hundred years ago, when the bombs were knocking out the country? Or maybe even a few years before that, when there were a hundred and eighty million people around, three times as many as now? Think of it – a hundred and eighty million slobs, jamming all the cities, crowding the streets and highways with their lousy, stinking automobiles?

'The Good Old Days, huh? What a laugh that was! Why, the first model hadn't been invented yet. A young fellow like you wouldn't be able to afford more than one flesh-and-blood female, and you'd work like a dog all your life just trying to support her. No extras, no new models, no trade-in, nothing! I'm not knocking flesh females, now, don't get me wrong – I've had a wife myself for fifteen years and we get along together swell. But think of what kind of a life it would be if that's all I had. Or all you had. Knocking yourself out just to keep body and soul together in some crummy sales job.'

Harrigan paused, then spoke solemnly. 'Just think about this for a minute, kid. You know what you'd probably be doing if you were alive back in the twentieth century? You'd be selling automobiles, that's what. How'd you like that, huh? Imagine being a car salesman – preying on the vanity of a bunch of old men and rich snobs, or swindling some poor guy out of his last buck with a used clunker.

'Just thank God you've got a chance to get into an honest line of business, where you can give the customer some real service and an honest return for his money.'

'I never thought of it that way,' Phil murmured.

'Well, you think about it now,' Harrigan told him. 'I'm going back to my office. You make up your mind what you're going to do. If you want to try the job out, you can start right away. If not, you can shove off. It's up to you.'

'I – I think maybe I'll give it a whirl.'

'Suit yourself.' Harrigan started walking away. 'But remember one thing – you have to change your attitude. In this business we wheel and deal, understand?'

He continued on into his office, without looking back. For an hour or so he busied himself at his desk, and it was almost noon when he strolled out onto the Used Model lot again.

There was young Phil, over in the corner, looming over a battered blonde 70 model that Harrigan remembered picking up from a one-day rental service. He had removed the covering from the nylon hair and he was gesturing earnestly to a small, rabbity-looking man who had all the earmarks of a hesitant customer. Harrigan could hear his vibrant voice even at a distance.

'Book value?' Phil was saying. 'Never mind about the book value. This one doesn't use any oil at all. I happen to know about this baby, Mister. You see, she belonged to an elderly school teacher, and he only used to take her out on Sundays—'

Mr. Harrigan smiled and quietly tiptoed away.

YOU GOT TO HAVE BRAINS

MUST have been about a year ago, give or take a month when Mr. Goofy first showed up here on the street.

We get all kinds here, you know — thousands of bums and winos floating in and out every day of the year. Nobody knows where they come from and nobody cares where they go. They sleep in flophouses, sleep in bars, and in doorways — sleep right out in the gutter if you let 'em. Just so's they get their kicks. Wine jags, shot-an'-beers, canned heat, reefers — there was one guy, he used to go around and bust up thermometers and drink the juice, so help me!

When you work behind the bar, like me, you get so you hardly notice people any more. But this Mr. Goofy was different.

He come in one night in winter, and the joint was almost empty. Most of the regulars, right after New Year's, they get themselves jugged and do ninety. Keeps 'em out of the cold.

So it was quiet when Mr. Goofy showed up, around supper time. He didn't come to the bar, even though he was all alone. He headed straight for a back booth, plunks down, and asked Ferd for a couple of hamburgers. That's when I noticed him.

What's so screwy about that? Well, it's because he was lugging about ten or fifteen pounds of scrap metal with him, that's why. He banged it down in the booth alongside him and sat there with his hands held over it like he was one of them guards at Fort Knox or wherever.

I mean, he had all this here dirty scrap metal — tin and steel and twisted old engine parts covered with mud. He must have dug it out of the dumps around Canal Street, some place like that. So when I got a chance I come down to this end of the bar and looked this character over. He sure was a sad one.

He was only about five feet high and weighed about a hunnerd pounds, just a little dried-up futz of a guy. He had a kind of bald head and he wore old twisted-up glasses with the earpieces all bent, and he had trouble with the hamburgers on account of his false choppers. He was dressed in them War Surplus things – leftovers from World War I, yet. And a cap.

Go out on the street right now and you'll see plenty more just like him, but Mr. Goofy was different. Because he was clean. Sure, he looked beat-up, but even his old duds was neat.

Another thing. While he waited for the hamburgers he kept writing stuff. He had this here pencil and notebook out and he was scribbling away for dear life. I got the idea he was figuring out some kind of arithametics.

Well, I was all set to ask him the score when somebody come in and I got busy. It happens that way; next thing I know the whole place was crowded and I forgot all about Mr. Goofy for maybe two hours. Then I happened to look over and by gawd if he ain't still sitting there, with that pencil going like crazy!

Only by this time the old juke is blasting, and he kind of frowns and takes his time like he didn't care for music but was, you know, concentrated on his figures, like.

He sees me watching him and wiggles his fingers like so, and I went over there and he says, 'Pardon me – but could you lower the volume of that instrument?'

Just like that he says it, with a kind of funny accent I can't place. But real polite and fancy for a foreigner.

So I says, 'Sure, I'll switch it down a little.' I went over and fiddled with the control to cut it down, like we do late at night.

But just then Stakowsky come up to me. This Stakowsky used to be a wheel on the street – owned two-three flop-houses and fleabag hotels, and he comes in regular to get loaded. He was kind of mean, but a good spender.

Well, Stakowsky come up and he stuck his big red face over the bar and yelled. 'Whassa big idea, Jack? I puts in my nickel,

I wanna hear my piece. You wanna busted nose or something?'

Like I say, he was a mean type.

I didn't know right off what to tell him, but it turned out I didn't have to tell him nothing. Because the little guy in the booth stood up and he tapped Stakowsky on the shoulder and said, real quiet, 'Pardon me, but it was I who requested that the music be made softer.'

Stakowsky turned around and he said, 'Yeah? And who in hell you think you are – somebody?'

The little guy said, 'You know me. I rented the top of the loft from you yesterday.'

Stakowsky looks at him again and then he says, 'Awright. So you rent. So you pay a month advance. Awright. But that ain't got to do with how I play music. I want it should be turned up, so me and my friends can hear it good.'

By this time the number is over and half the bar has come down to get in on the deal. They was all standing around waiting for the next pitch.

The little guy says, 'You don't understand, Mr. Stakowsky. It happens I am doing some very important work and require freedom from distraction.'

I bet Stakowsky never heard no two-dollar words before. He got redder and redder and at last he says, 'You don't understand so good, neither. You wanna figure, go by your loft. Now I turn up the music. Are you gonna try and stop me?' And he takes a swipe at the little futz with his fist.

Little guy never batted an eye. He just sort of ducked, and when he come up again he had a shiv in his hand. But it wasn't no regular shiv, and it wasn't nothing he found in no junk-heap.

This one was about a foot long, and sharp. The blade was sharp and the tip was sharp, and the little guy didn't look like he was just gonna give Stakowsky a shave with it.

Stakowsky, he didn't think so either. He whitened up fast and backed away to the bar and he says, 'All right, all right,' over and over again.

It happened all in a minute, and then the knife was gone and the little guy picked up his scrap metal and walked out without even looking back once.

Then everybody was hollering, and I poured Stakowsky a fast double, and then another. Of course he made off like he hadn't been scared and he talked plenty loud – but we all knew.

'Goofy,' he says. 'That's who he is. Mr. Goofy. Sure, he rents from me. You know, by the Palace Rooms, where I live. He rents the top – a great big loft up there. Comes yesterday, a month rent in advance he pays too. I tell him, "Mister, you're goofy. What do you want with such a big empty loft? A loft ain't no good in winter, unless you want to freeze. Why you don't take a nice warm room downstairs by the steam heat?" But no, he wants the loft, and I should put up a cot for him. So I do, and he moves in last night.'

Stakowsky got red in the face. 'All day today that Mr. Goofy, he's bringing up his crazy outfits. Iron and busted machinery. Stuff like that. I ask him what he's doing and he says he's building. I ask him what he's building and he says – well, he just don't say. You saw how he acted tonight? Now you know. He's goofy in the head. I ain't afraid of no guys, but those crazy ones you got to watch out for. Lofts and machinery and knives – you ever hear anything like that Mr. Goofy?'

So that's how he got his name. And I remembered him. One of the reasons was, I was staying at the Palace Rooms myself. Not in the flops, but a nice place on the third floor, right next to Stakowsky's room. And right upstairs from us was this loft. An attic, like. I never went up there, but there were stairs in back.

The next couple of days I kept my eyes open, figuring on seeing Mr. Goofy again. But I didn't. All I did was hear him. Nights, he kept banging and pounding away, him and his scrap metal or whatever it was, and he moved stuff across the floor. Me, I'm a pretty sound sleeper and Stakowsky was always loaded when he turned in, so it didn't bother him neither. But Mr. Goofy never seemed to sleep. He was always working up there. And on what?

I couldn't figure it out. Day after day he'd come in and out with some more metal. I don't know where he got it all, but he must have lugged up a couple of thousand pounds, ten or fifteen each trip. It got to bothering me because it was the sort of a mystery you feel you've got to know more about.

Next time I saw him was when he started coming into the place regular, to eat. And always he had the pencil and notebook with him. He took the same booth every night – and nobody bothered him with loud music after the story got around about him and his shiv.

He'd just sit there and figure and mumble to himself and walk out again, and pretty soon they were making up all kinds of stories about the guy.

Some said he was a Red on account of that accent, you know, and he was building one of them there atomic bombs. One of the winos says no, he passed the place one night about four A.M. and he heard a big clank like machinery working. He figured Mr. Goofy was a counter-fitter. Which was the kind of crazy idea you'd expect from a wino.

Anyways, the closest anybody come was Manny Schreiber from the hock shop, and he guessed Goofy was a inventor and maybe he was building a rowbot. You know, a rowbot, like in these scientist magazines. Mechanical men, they run by machinery.

One day, about an hour before I went on shift, I was sitting in my room when Stakowsky knocked on the door. 'Come on,' he says. 'Mr. Goofy just went out. I'm gonna take a look around up there.'

Well, I didn't care one way or the other. Stakowsky, he was the landlord, and I figured he had a right. So we sneaked up and he used his key and we went inside the loft.

It was a big barn of a place with a cot in the corner. Next to the cot was a table with a lot of notes piled up, and maybe twenty-five or thirty books. Foreign books they were, and I couldn't make out the names. In the other corners there were piles of scrap metal and what looked like a bunch of old radio sets from a repair shop.

And in the center of the room was this machine. At least, it looked like a machine, even though it must have been thirty feet long. It was higher than my head, too. And there was a door in it, and you could get inside the machinery that was all tangled up on the sides and sit down in a chair. In front of the chair was a big board with a lot of switches on it.

And everywhere was gears and pistons and coils and even glass tubes. Where he picked up all that stuff, I dunno. But he'd patched it all together somehow and when you looked at it – it made sense. I mean, you could tell the machine would do something, if you could only figure out what.

Stakowsky looked at me and I looked at him and we both looked at the machine.

'That Mr. Goofy!' says Stakowsky. 'He does all this in a month. You know something, Jack?'

'What?' I says.

'You tell anybody else and I'll kill you. But I'm scared to even come near Mr. Goofy. This machine of his, I don't like it. Tomorrow his month is up. I'm going to tell him he should move. Get out. I don't want crazy people around here.'

'But how'll he move this thing out?'

'I don't care how. Tomorrow he gets the word. And I'm going to have Lippy and Stan and the boys here. He don't pull no knife on me again. Out he goes.'

We went downstairs and I went to work. All night long I tried to figure that machine of his. There wasn't much else to do, because there was a real blizzard going and nobody came in.

I kept remembering the way the machine looked. It had a sort of framework running around the outside, and if it got covered over with some metal it would be like a submarine or one of them rockets. And there was a part inside, where a big glass globe connected up to some wires leading to the switch-board, or whatever it was. And a guy could sit in there. It all made some kind of crazy sense.

I sat there, thinking it over, until along about midnight. Then Mr. Goofy came in.

This time he didn't head for his booth. He come right up to the bar and sat down on a stool. His face was red, and he brushed snow off his coat. But he looked happy.

'Do you have any decent brandy?' he asked.

'I think so,' I told him. I found a bottle and opened it up.

'Will you be good enough to have a drink with me?'

'Sure, thanks.' I looked at him. 'Celebrating?'

'That's right,' says Mr. Goofy. 'This is a great occasion. My work is finished. Tonight I put on the sheaths. Now I am almost ready to demonstrate.'

'Demonstrate what?'

Well, he dummied up on me right away. I poured him another drink and another, and he just sat there grinning. Then he sort of loosened up. That brandy was plenty powerful.

'Look,' he says. 'I will tell you all about it. You have been kind to me, and I can trust you. Besides, it is good to share a moment of triumph.'

He says, 'So long I have worked, but soon they will not laugh at me any more. Soon the smart Americans, the men over here who call themselves Professors, will take note of my work. They did not believe me when I offered to show them my plans. They would not accept my basic theory. But I knew I was right. I knew I could do it. Part of it must be mechanical, yes. But the most important part is the mind itself. You know what I told them? To do this, and to do it right, you've got to have brains.'

He sort of chuckled, and poured another drink. 'Yes. That is the whole secret. More than anything else, you need brains. Not mechanical formula alone. But when I spoke of harnessing the mind, powering it with metal energy rather than physical, they laughed. Now we'll see.'

I brought myself a drink, and I guess he realized I wasn't in on the pitch, because he says, 'You don't understand, do you?'

I shook my head.

'What would you say, my friend, if I told you I have just successfully completed the construction of the first practical spaceship?'

Oh-oh, I thought to myself. Mr. Goofy!

'But not a model, not a theory in metal – an actual, practical machine for travel to the moon?'

Mr. Goofy and his knife, I thought. Making a crazy thing out of old scrap iron. Mr. Goofy!

'If I wish, I can go tonight,' he said. 'Or tomorrow. Any time. No astronomy. No calculus. Mental energy is the secret. Harness the machinery to a human brain and it will be guided automatically to its destination in a moment, if properly controlled. That's all it takes – a single instant. Long enough to direct the potential energy of the cortex.'

Maybe you think it's funny the way I can remember all those big words, but I'll never forget anything Mr. Goofy said.

And he told me, 'Who has ever estimated the power of the human brain – its unexploited capacity for performance? Using the machine for autohypnosis, the brain is capable of tremendous effort. The electrical impulses can be stepped up, magnified ten millionfold. Atomic energy is insignificant in comparison. Now do you see what I have achieved?'

I thought about it for a minute or so – him sitting there all steamed up over his dizzy junk heap. Then I remembered what was happening to him tomorrow.

I just didn't have the heart to let him go on and on about how his life-work was realized, and how he'd be famous in Europe and America and he'd reach the moon and all that crud. I didn't have the heart. He was so little and so whacky. Mr. Goofy!

So I says, 'Look, I got to tell you something. Stakowsky, he's bouncing you out tomorrow. That's right. He's gonna kick you and your machine into the street. He says he can't stand it around.'

'Machine?' says Mr. Goofy. 'What does he know of my machine?'

Well, I had to tell him then. I had to. About how we went upstairs and looked.

'Before the sheath was on, you saw?' he asked.

'That's the way it was,' I told him. 'I saw it, and so did Stakowsky. And he'll kick you out.'

'But he cannot! I mean, I chose this spot carefully, so I could work unobserved. I need privacy. And I cannot move the ship now. I must bring people to see it when I make the announcement. I must make the special arrangements for the tests. It is a very delicate matter. Doesn't he understand? He'll be famous, too, because of what happened in his miserable hole of a place—'

'He's probably famous tonight,' I said. 'I'll bet he's down the street somewheres right now, babbling about you and your machine, and how he's gonna toss you out.'

Mr. Goofy looked so sad I tried to make a joke. 'What's the matter with you? You say yourself it works by brain power. So use your brain and move it some place else. Huh?'

He looked even sadder. 'Don't you realize it is designed only for space-travel? And properly, my brain must be free to act as the control agent. Still, you are right about that man. He is a wicked person, and he hates me. I must do something. I wonder if—'

Then you know what he does, this Mr. Goofy? He whips out his pencil and notebook and starts figuring. Just sits there and scribbles away. And he says, 'Yes, it is possible. Change the wires leading to the controls. It is only a matter of a few moments. And what better proof could I ask than an actual demonstration? Yes. It is fated to be this way, Good.'

Then he stood up and stuck out his mitt. 'Good-by, Jack,' he says. 'And thank you for your suggestion.'

'What suggestion?'

But he doesn't answer me, and then he's out the door and gone.

I closed up the joint about one-thirty. The boss wasn't around and I figured what the hell, it was a blizzard.

There was nobody out on the street this time of night, not

with the wind off the lake and the snow coming down about a foot a minute. I couldn't see in front of my face.

I crossed the street in front of the Palace Rooms – it must have been quarter to two or thereabouts – and all of a sudden it happened.

Whoom!

Like that it goes, a big loud blast you can hear even over the wind and the blizzard. On account of the snow being so thick I couldn't see nothing. But let me tell you. I sure heard it.

At first I thought maybe it was some kind of explosion, so I quick run across to the Palace and up the stairs. All the winos in the flops was asleep – those guys, they get a jag on and they'll sleep even if you set fire to the mattress. But I had to find out if anything was wrong.

I didn't smell no smoke and my room was okay, and it was all quiet in the hall. Except that the back door leading to the attic was open, and the air was cold.

Right away I figured maybe Mr. Goofy had pulled something off, so I ran up the stairs. And I saw it.

Mr. Goofy was gone. The junk was still scattered all over the room, but he'd burned all his notes and he was gone. The great big machine, or spaceship, or whatever it was – that was gone, too.

How'd he get it out of the room and where did he take it? You can search me, brother.

All I know is there was a big charred spot burned away in the center of the floor where the machine had stood. And right above there was a big round hole punched smack through the roof of the loft.

So help me, I just stood there. What else could I do? Mr. Goofy said he built a spaceship that could take him to the moon. He said he could go there in a flash, just like that. He said all it took was brains.

And what do I know about this here autohypnosis deal, or whatever he called it, and about electricity-energy, and force fields, and all that stuff?

He was gone. The machine or ship was gone. And there was this awful hole in the roof. That's all I knew.

Maybe Stakowsky would know the rest. It was worth a try, anyhow. So I run down to Stakowsky's room.

After that, things didn't go so good.

The cops started to push me around when they got there, and if it hadn't been for my boss putting the old pressure on, they'd have given me a real rough time. But they could see I was sorta like out of my head – and I was, too, for about a week.

I kept yelling about this Mr. Goofy and his crazy invention and his big knife and his trip to the moon, and it didn't make no sense to the cops. Of course, nothing ever made any sense to them, and they had to drop the whole case – hush it up. The whole thing was too screwy to ever let leak out.

Anyhow, I felt rugged until I moved out of the Palace Rooms and got back to work. Now I scarcely ever think about Mr. Goofy any more, or Stakowsky – or the whole cockeyed mess.

I don't like to think about the mess.

The mess was when I ran down the stairs that night and looked for Stakowsky in his room. He was there all right, but he didn't care about Goofy or the trip to the moon or the hole in his loft roof, either.

Because he was very, very dead.

And Mr. Goofy's foot-long knife was laying right next to him on the bed. So that part was easy to figure out. Mr. Goofy come right back there from the tavern, and he killed him.

But after that?

After that, your guess is as good as mine. The cops never found out a bit – not even Mr. Goofy's real name, or where he came from, or where he got this here theory about spaceships and power to run them.

Did he really have a invention that would take him to the moon? Could he change some wires and controls and just scoot off through the roof with his mental energy hooked up?

Nobody knows. Nobody ever will know. But I can tell you this.

There was a mess, one awful mess, in Stakowsky's room. Mr. Goofy must have taken his knife and gone to work on Stakowsky's head. There was nothing left on top but a big round hole, and it was empty.

Stakowsky's head was empty.

Mr. Goofy took out what was inside and fixed his machine and went to the moon.

That's all.

Like Mr. Goofy says, you got to have brains. . .

YOU COULD BE WRONG

WHEN Harry Jessup came back from service, he wasn't aware of the change. Not immediately.

Marge was still waiting for him, so they got married and bought a little ranch house out in Skyland Park. Harry got a job at Everlift, and although he noticed money didn't seem to go very far these days, he managed to get along. He and Marge made friends with the couple next door – the Myers, very nice people; Ed Myers was a CPA – and pretty soon they bought a television set.

That's probably what set him off.

One night he and Marge were watching the Sloucho Marks quiz show. Harry had always liked Sloucho in the old days, when he was making pictures, and he could still quote most of the lyrics to 'Hooray For Captain Mauldin.'

Marge kept laughing at Sloucho's cracks during the program, and she was a little surprised to see that Harry was just sitting there, staring at the screen. He never smiled. When it was time for the last commercial, Harry got up and turned off the set.

'What's the matter?' Marge asked.

Harry muttered something that sounded like, 'Fake!' but Marge wasn't really interested in his reply. She'd asked a purely rhetorical question and intended to follow it up with certain remarks which she now delivered.

'I thought it was a very funny show, myself,' she said. 'What's wrong with you, Harry? You always liked Sloucho Marks before.'

'Yeah,' Harry said. He just sat there, staring at the blank screen.

'You've got to admit he's the cleverest ad-libber in the world,' Marge persisted. 'Maybe he's a little corny, but I'd like to see you do any better, Harry Jessup.'

Harry scowled at her. 'Perhaps I could,' he murmured, 'if I had four writers.'

'Four writers?' Marge was genuinely shocked. 'What are you talking about?'

'He's got four writers,' Harry said. 'I read about it in the paper.'

Marge sniffed. 'Why, I never heard of such a ridiculous idea! Everybody knows it wouldn't work. How can anybody write such a show in advance when they don't know who's going to be chosen as contestants?'

'They know,' Harry told her. 'It's all fixed in advance. Re-hearsals and everything.'

'Nonsense!'

'Some of the people who are going to be on the show even advertise ahead of time in the Hollywood trade papers,' Harry said.

'Who told you that?'

'Read it.'

'Well, I don't believe a word of it,' Marge declared. 'I think you're just jealous, or something. I bet you wouldn't mind trading places with Sloucho Marks any day.'

'Maybe I could,' Harry answered.

'What are you talking about?' Marge sat down heavily and began tapping her foot.

'I mean, maybe I could be Sloucho Marks,' Harry said. 'How do you know you're seeing the real Sloucho on TV now?'

'Oh, don't be ridiculous! Just because he's given up wearing that false moustache—'

'Did you ever see him before without it? I mean, outside of his last movies where he appeared alone?'

'No, – but—'

'Maybe there isn't a real Sloucho,' Harry persisted. 'Maybe there never was. Remember in one of his early movies where he stood in front of this mirror frame and thought there was glass in it? And Cheeko put on a moustache and pretended to be his reflection? Cheeko looked just like Sloucho. Anybody can, with a little make-up.'

'What's come over you, Harry?'

'Nothing. It just occurred to me how easy it would be to pull off a stunt like that nowadays. Anybody with four writers and a physical resemblance could act the part. The whole thing's a fake from start to finish. A pretended ad-libber purporting to interview phony contestants in a comedy show which is supposed to be a quiz program. All a big fraud.'

'I don't understand why you're getting so riled up over nothing,' Marge snapped. 'If you get right down to it, Sloucho certainly didn't write all his own parts in the old days.'

'Of course not.' Harry sighed. 'But nobody ever tried to pretend he did. When you saw him on the stage or in the movies, you knew it was make-believe. Now they try to get you to think it's real. That's what bothers me.'

'But it is real. You saw it!'

Harry Jessup shook his head. 'No I didn't. And neither did you. All we saw was a wave-pattern, reproduced. You don't really see a picture on TV; your eyes merely interpret it that way. Same as moving pictures – they don't move. I was reading all about it in—'

Marge sniffed again. 'Did it ever occur to your precious intellect that maybe what you read is phony, too? Just because its printed somewhere, that's no reason you have to believe it any more than if you saw it.'

Harry blinked. 'I never thought of that angle before.'

Marge saw her advantage and pursued it. 'Well, suppose you think about it before you sound off any more. How do you know it's true Sloucho has four writers? That could be a lie, too.' She smiled triumphantly.

'Yes.' Harry didn't smile back. 'Yes, it could be, couldn't it? But why – that's what I want to know. What's the meaning of it?' He paused and stared down at Marge's foot.

Marge noticed his stare and stopped tapping. 'Sorry,' she said. 'Didn't mean to get on your nerves.'

'Well, it does,' Harry declared. 'I wish you wouldn't wear those heels. You're five-feet-two. Why must you pretend to be five-feet-four?'

Marge went over and put her hand on Harry's forehead. When she spoke, her voice was soft. 'What's gotten into you?' she asked. 'Don't you feel well?'

Harry reached up and clasped her hand. He pulled it down to eye-level. 'Nail polish,' he muttered. 'Pretending you have red nails. Don't understand it.'

'You're sick. You've got a fever—' Marge rose. 'I'll get the thermometer and we'll see.'

He shook his head. 'I don't need any thermometer.'

Marge decided to humor him. 'Just for fun,' she said. 'After all, it's a brand-new one. I just bought it, and we might as well get some use out of it.'

'New one. That's just the trouble. It might be a phony, too. Built to register fever when there isn't any.'

'Harry!'

'I'm going to bed.' He stood up and shuffled over to the door. 'You asked what's gotten into me,' he said. 'I don't know. Maybe it's honesty.'

Marge knew better. Harry had a fever, all right. He went to work Friday, but when he came home his face was flushed and his eyes were red. He didn't say very much, either.

They sat down to eat, and Harry stared at his plate. 'What's this?' he asked in a harsh voice.

'Mock chicken legs.'

'Mock chicken?' Harry pushed his plate away. 'Why can't we have real chicken for a change?'

'I don't know, I just thought—'

Harry was looking over the table now, muttering to himself. 'White bread. You know how they make white bread these days? Take all the nourishment out and then fortify it artificially with vitamins. Oleo instead of butter. Process cheese. That's synthetic, too. And instant coffee—'

'But you know how much regular coffee costs nowadays, dear.'

'Doesn't matter. Suppose it was beer instead of coffee. Same thing. Brewed with chemicals instead of the old way. Even the water isn't water any more – it's something filled with chlorine and fluorine and heaven only knows what.'

Harry pushed back his chair.

'Where are you going?'

'Out for a walk.'

Marge drew in her breath. 'You aren't going down to the tavern?'

He made a barking sound, then caught himself. 'What's the matter with me?' he said. 'Can't I even come up with a genuine laugh any more? It's getting me fast, the thing's contagious, isn't it?'

'Harry, you promised you wouldn't go to that tavern—'

'Don't worry about me.' He smiled. 'Tavern! It isn't a tavern, it's a saloon. No such thing as a real tavern, you know. Just a name they use to make it sound fancy. In a real tavern you used to be able to drink whisky. Nowadays you get something called a blend – 65 per cent or 72 per cent neutral spirits, artificially aged in imitation-charred casks. Fake!'

Marge came over to him, but he pushed her away, 'Why do you use perfume?' he asked. 'You don't smell that way, really.'

'Lie down,' she whispered. 'I'll call Doctor Lorentz.'

'Don't want a doctor. Just going for a walk. Got to think.' Harry looked at the wall. 'Quit my job today.'

'Quit your job?' She was suddenly tense. 'Why?'

'Tired of it. Tired of making brassieres. Falsies. That's what they call them and that's what they are – false. I want to get into something real.'

He backed over to the door. 'Don't worry. We'll work things out. I'll figure a way, if there is a way.'

Then he was gone.

For a moment, Marge watched him through the window, then bit her lip and hurried to the telephone.

Harry came back in about an hour. Marge met him at the door.

'Feel better, dear?' she asked.

'Yeah.' He patted her shoulder. 'I'm all right.'

'Good.' She smiled. 'Ed Myers is in the living room.'

'What's he doing here?'

'Just dropped in to visit. Thought he'd like to talk to you, I guess.'

'You guess!' Harry stepped back. 'You told him to come over, didn't you?'

'Well—'

'Lies,' he muttered. 'All lies. Oh, what the hell, I'll see him.'

He strode into the living room.

'Hello, Harry,' said Ed Myers. Myers was a big, blond, jolly, fat man with round baby-blue eyes. He sat there in the easy chair, puffing on a cigarette.

'Hi,' Harry said. 'Want a drink?'

'No, thanks. Just dropped in for a minute.'

Harry sat down and Myers grinned amiably. 'How's tricks?' he asked.

'Tricks! It's all tricks.'

'What's that?'

'You heard me. You ought to know. You and this "just dropped in for a minute" routine. Marge called you over, didn't she?'

'Well—'

'What did she tell you?' Harry leaned forward, his expression angry.

'Nothing, really. That is, she said you'd been sort of under the weather lately. Figured there might be something on your mind you'd like to talk about. And seeing as how I'm a friend of yours—'

'Are you?'

'You know that, pal.'

'Do I? I'm beginning to wonder if I know anything. Maybe that's it – I didn't know, but I'm starting to find out.'

'I don't get it, Harry.'

'Just took a walk. Walked around the block a couple of times, then down to the corner. What did I see?'

'You got me, pal. What did you see?'

'Fakes. Phonies. Frauds.'

'This doesn't sound like you, Harry.'

'How do you know what I sound like? Really, I mean?' Harry Jessup bit his lip. 'Listen, and I'll try to explain. I walk down the street and I look back at this house. This house – what is it? They call it a "ranch house". Why? It's not on a ranch. It's not the kind of a house anybody ever built on a real ranch. Just a five-room crackerbox with a fake gable in front and a fake chimney to indicate a non-existent fireplace. This neighborhood is full of them. A thousand neighborhoods are full of them. Must be five, maybe ten million such places built in the last few years.'

'So why get excited over a thing like that?'

'I'm not excited. Just curious. About a lot of things. Skyland Park, for instance. That's the name of this suburb, isn't it? But it's not a park, and there's no view of the sky around here. Everything's blotted out by TV aerials. People sitting in the dark, watching something that's not real, but pretending to themselves that it is.'

Ed Myers chuckled. 'Marge told me about Sloucho Marks,' he said. 'Mean to say you let a little thing like that get on your nerves?'

'It isn't a little thing, Ed. At least, I don't think so. Everything's like that nowadays. I didn't understand at first when I came back, but I get the picture now. I got it tonight. The TV all over, and men standing outside washing their cars. Hundreds of average men, but none of them own an average car.'

'How's that again?'

'Ever stop to think about that, Ed? No average cars any

99

more. Everybody's got a Commander, or a Land Cruiser, or a Coup de Ville, or a Roadmaster, or a Champion. Even the poorest slob owns a Super Deluxe Model. Aren't there any plain, old-fashioned automobiles any more? I haven't seen any. Just millions of Hornets and Ambassadors and Strato-jets, driven by people who have no place to go. No real place, that is. They drive to a grocery store built like an Italian Doge's palace which calls itself a Supermarket and offers Below Cost Bargains, yet still makes a profit, and—'

'Dig this!' Ed Myers chuckled again. 'You talk like a Commie.'

'How do you know how a Commie talks?' Harry retorted. 'You ever hear one? Did you ever see one in the flesh?'

'Why, no, but I read the papers; everybody knows about Communists.'

'You mean everybody is told about them. You read what's printed, that's all. How do you know any of it ever happened?'

'Hey, wait a minute, Harry!'

'You read about the President's latest speech, but he didn't write it – some team of ghost writers ground it out. You read about the war, and what you read is censored. You read about some movie star, and it turns out to be a planted publicity story, concerning an interview that never occurred. How do you ever know what actually happens? Or if anything is actually happening?'

'Say, you are serious, aren't you?'

'I don't know. I walked and walked tonight trying to figure things out. Nothing makes sense. Ed, I saw the kids in the street. Little kids running around playing cops and robbers, cowboys and Indians, playing war. It scared me.'

'Why should it scare you, pal? Didn't you do those things when you were a kid?'

'Sure. Of course I did. But I didn't play the same way. I knew it was a game, just make-believe. I'm not so sure about the kids today. I swear, from the way they act, they think it's real.'

'Harry, you're making a mountain out of a molehill.'

'That's the fashion, isn't it? If I really knew how, I could become quite wealthy in these times. Anybody who can take a molehill and persuade people into thinking it's a mountain is right in style. Look at that!'

Ed Myers was lighting another cigarette, but Harry snatched it out of his mouth.

'Here you are,' he said. 'Perfect example. The world's finest tobacco, isn't it? Mildest, choicest, most expensive blend. That's how it's advertised. Do you believe it? Do you realize there are a hundred brands that cost more, taste better?'

'But everybody knows about advertising—'

'I'm not talking about advertising. It used to be bad enough, when advertising was the only big offender. But things like this are happening all over. We're losing the truth, Ed. The truth about everything. Politics, government, world affairs, business, education – we get it all through a filter, selected and distorted. Where has reality disappeared to?'

'You're getting yourself all worked up over nothing,' Ed Myers said. 'What you need is a vacation, little relaxation.'

'Relaxation? How? I watched television last Sunday. Jack Benny. He did a show which was supposed to take place ten minutes before he went on the air. In the middle of the program he pretended he was going on the air and got himself introduced all over again. Then in a few minutes, during the pretended show, he was supposed to go over to visit the home of a cast member. By this time I couldn't even follow what he was pretending to pretend.'

'Movies are worse. Did you ever see that oldie, "Jolson Sings Again"? Larry Parks plays Jolson, of course, but Jolson did the singing. That's par for the course these days. But then, in the middle of the picture, Parks as Jolson is supposed to meet Parks as Parks. And he plays both parts. Parks-Jolson talks to Parks-Parks about making a picture of Jolson's life, and then the picture of Jolson's life goes on to show how a picture of

Jolson's life was made. Only what is shown isn't what really happened to begin with, so—'

'Calm down, boy!' Myers grinned. 'It's all in fun.'

'I'm calm, but I'm not so sure about the fun part. Not any more. This is getting serious. I happen to like real things. And everything is ersatz.'

'You're just picking out a few examples and magnifying them all out of proportion.'

'Proportion? How do we know what proportion is? You've got to have something to measure against. Pontius Pilate asked "What is Truth?" I'm still worried about the answer.'

'Well, if you want to drag religion into it—'

'I'm not dragging religion into it. Look at yourself, for example.' Harry Jessup was on his feet now, almost shouting. 'You're wearing a sports jacket. You a sportsman by any chance? No. Examine those pearl buttons. Are they made of pearl? Not on your life. That gold watchband – it's not gold is it? Regimental stripe tie. You ever belong to the Coldstream Guards? Your shoes, with the leather heels that you aren't even conscious of any more. CPA, that's your job. Filling out fake income tax returns for fake businessmen who contribute sums for fictitious government expenditures—'

'Harry, you're shouting!' Marge came into the room. 'What's wrong?'

'Everything.' He went over to her now and his finger stabbed again and again. He talked for Ed Myers' benefit. 'Look at her. Blonde, curly hair. Know why? Bleach and a permanent wave. Two false teeth in front. Foundation garment to disguise her shape. Been married to her for almost a year, and I swear I've never seen her real face – just a lot of make-up. Make-up and fake mannerisms, that's all she is!'

Marge started to cry. 'You see,' she sobbed. 'That's what I meant. He's been like this ever since last night.'

Ed Myers wasn't smiling any more. He nodded gravely. 'Maybe we ought to call some specialist and—'

'Wait a minute,' Harry said. 'Wait a minute! You think I'm

cracking up, don't you? You think I'm real gone in the head.'

Myers shrugged. He didn't say anything.

'All right.' Harry lowered his voice with an effort. 'All right. Maybe I'd better tell you the rest.'

'The rest?' Marge stopped sniffling. Ed Myers hunched forward, picking at his ear.

'Yeah. I never said anything about it before, because I thought it was just a lot of malarkey when I heard it. Now I'm not so sure.'

'Heard what?' Myers asked.

'About the bombs.' Harry took a deep breath. 'Last year, when I was in service abroad, this rumor came along. Nobody ever found out how it started. Anyway, we all heard it. According to the way it went, the Russians came over and bombed the United States. Bombed hell out of it. That was one story. At the same time, we heard another. This one was different. According to the second rumor, it wasn't the Russians at all. Some of our own scientists came up with a new kind of bomb. They tested it, but there was a chain-reaction, a big one. Blew up the whole damn' country!'

'A specialist—' Myers began.

'Wait. Let me finish. Then you can call your specialist, if you want to. Somebody ought to be able to give me an answer.'

Marge came over to Harry and put her hand on his arm. 'Listen to me, Harry,' she said. 'Are you trying to tell me you think the country was destroyed while you were in service?'

'I don't know,' he muttered. 'I don't know what I'm trying to tell you, or myself, either.'

'Be reasonable, Harry. Think for a moment. You're here, aren't you? And so are we. We're in this country. So how could it be destroyed? Do you see any ruins, any signs of bombing?'

'No. But I wouldn't. Not if all the real things were gone and the fakes remained. You can't destroy what actually doesn't exist.'

Ed Myers stood up. He glanced significantly at Marge. 'Let me use your phone,' he said.

Marge waved her hand. 'Wait. Not yet. Give him a chance to explain.'

'Thanks.' Harry smiled up at her gratefully. 'You know, this business of seeing things proves nothing. They say when you're born, you see things upside down. I don't understand it, but the image is supposed to be received on the retina that way, and then translated by the brain so that you think it's right-side up. The whole business of seeing is cockeyed, anyhow. This thing that looks like a table, as I remember it, is just trillions and trillions of little particles jumping up and down in waves. All our senses are playing tricks on us; smell, hearing, everything. Lots of people get hallucinations—'

'Don't they, though?' Myers glanced again at Marge, and picked at his right ear once more.

'Please,' Marge whispered.

Harry went on. 'So maybe none of us ever comes close to Reality, after all. We just sort of agree amongst ourselves that certain things are real and certain things are not real. We base those agreements on the evidence of our senses; if we all get just about the same reactions, we decide to believe or disbelieve accordingly. You follow me?'

'I think so,' Marge said. 'But doesn't that prove you're living in a real world?'

'Not any more. Not since this phony stuff took over, the way it has in the last ten years or so. I said our senses can play tricks. Maybe they've gotten so used to the fakes they can't detect the difference any more. Maybe there's a sort of balancing point somewhere. As long as 50 per cent of our environment is real, we're safe. We can still recognize it, use it as a gauge to judge our surroundings. But when there isn't 50 per cent left – when more than half of the things we see, or hear, or say, or do, or own, or experience are false – then how can we tell? Maybe we reached that point a long time ago and didn't know it. Maybe we're all hypnotized into believing in the existence of a lot of things. If that was so, then the real world could actually disappear and we'd never even suspect it. Because all the illusions we've come to think of as reality would still remain.'

'Sort of a mirage, eh?' Ed Myers nodded. 'You sure worked yourself up a theory, boy. But there's kind of a hole in it, isn't there?'

'Hole?'

'Well, just for the sake of argument, supposing something like that had happened. Let's even use that rumor you and the troops heard over in Asia, about how the whole country was knocked out by chain-reaction. Then how could you come back here again to live? There'd be nothing left, isn't that right? No people, no buildings, no radio, or TV, or books, or movies, or any of the stuff you're so badly worried about.'

'But if we believed it was here—' Harry started, then stopped. 'Come to think of it, I guess you're right.'

'Of course I'm right.' Myers smiled again. 'You just think about it a while, boy. Everything'll straighten out. Take a rest for a few days, you'll get over it.'

Marge smiled, too. 'You gave us an awful scare. Harry.'

'Scare?' Harry Jessup blinked. 'Scare? Could that be it?'

'Could what be what?'

'Scare. The flying saucers scare. Remember? We heard all about it. Sure – that could be the answer!'

'Oh, Harry, for heaven's sake—'

'Same deal. Nobody knew whether they were real or fake either. But suppose they were real. And they dropped the bombs. A new kind. Wiped out the country and took over. Nobody'd ever know. They'd send out fake reports, create an illusion that nothing had changed. People coming in from abroad would find everything the same. So accustomed to fakery in normal life, they wouldn't notice the difference. Just as I didn't notice.'

Ed Myers groaned. Marge sighed.

'That's the answer!' Harry cried. 'It has to be the answer! Nobody left at all, and the whole thing is an illusion built up to protect whoever or whatever owns this country now – built up to fool the real people left, the ones in Service who came back! They'll just have to keep things going until we're dead and buried and then the masquerade is over.

'No wonder they keep pouring out more and more synthetics all the time! Do it to deaden our faculties, get us so used to the artificial we'll forget there ever was anything real. Who remembers, when nobody had their teeth capped, when Wild Bill Hickok was an outlaw instead of a hero? Today kids think there really was a man named Sherlock Holmes – if there are any kids, that is.'

'Are any kids?' Marge shuddered. 'Do you know what you're saying now? Are you inferring that—?'

Harry paused. 'Yeah,' he said, slowly. 'Yeah. Come to think of it. I am.'

He walked over to Ed Myers, who was still picking his ear. Suddenly he reached out and grabbed at Myers, trying to reach the side of his head.

Myers ducked, moved back in alarm.

'That gray spot,' Harry whispered. 'I think I know what it is, now.'

'Keep away from me!' Ed Myers yelled.

But Harry didn't keep away. He lunged forward, grabbing up the paper-knife from the desk and bringing it down with a single, startling motion.

There was a ripping sound. Harry plunged the paper-knife into Myers' head.

'Look!' he shouted. 'I was right – nothing but sawdust! Sawdust and a bunch of cog-wheels.'

Myers fell to the floor and lay still.

Marge began to scream.

'Look!' Harry yelled. 'Sawdust, all over the rug! Can't you see—?'

He stopped. Marge kept staring at the floor, her scream subsiding to a whimper. 'Harry, you've killed him.'

'How could I kill something that isn't real? Something stuffed with sawdust?'

'Take another look,' Marge said. 'That isn't sawdust. It's blood.'

Harry took another look. The knife clattered to the floor. He stared down at the slowly widening red pool . . .

He was still staring when Marge went to the phone. He was still staring when she came back. He was still staring when the squad-car arrived.

After that there were questions, many questions, and a lot of men crowded around, and somebody came in with a camera and flashbulbs and took pictures, and then they took Ed Myers' body away, and finally they took Harry away too.

At the end, there was nobody left but Marge. She was all alone and there was nothing else to do, so she got out the dustpan and the broom and swept up the little pile of sawdust from the floor.

EGGHEAD

SHERRY was the first one to notice.

I picked her up in front of the sorority house about eight and I'll never forget the way her eyes got wide as she stared at me.

'Why, Dick!' she gasped. 'You are letting your hair grow!'

I couldn't help it. I turned red as a beet. 'Yeah,' I mumbled. 'Kinda looks that way, doesn't it?'

Her eyes got wider. 'And what's that you're wearing? I mean, *what* on *earth*?'

'It's a double-breasted suit,' I told her. 'Picked it up last weekend, when I went home. I figured it was sort of different.'

'Different? It's horrible! I'll bet nobody's worn one of those things in years.'

I shrugged. 'Sorry. But I thought, since we were only going to have breakfast together, it would not make much difference.' I didn't want to see her face, so I made a big production out of looking at my watch. 'Come on, it's after eight, and I've got a nine-o'clock this morning. We'd better hurry.'

She didn't answer. I took her arm and steered her into the drugstore on the corner. It was crowded, as usual, and the juke was going. The big screen was behind the counter, but there were smaller ones in most of the booths. Only the two little booths at the rear didn't have juke-screens, and of course they were vacant. Nobody wants to sit where you can't see the screens. Right now Buzzy Blake was doing Number One – the Extra-Cola commercial.

Sherry made a face. 'I suppose we'll just have to wait for a place,' she said.

'Haven't got time,' I told her. 'Let's grab a bite in one of the back booths.'

I sat her down before she could object, and pretty soon the waitress came up with two mugs of coffee.

'What'll it be?' she asked.

'Cruller,' Sherry said.

The waitress looked at me and I shook my head. 'No cruller. I want poached eggs. And you can take this coffee back, too. I didn't order it.'

'You don't want coffee?'

'I think I'd prefer cocoa instead.'

They were both staring at me. I wanted to sink right through the floor.

Sherry leaned over the table. 'Dick, what's wrong with you? Are you sick?'

'No, I'm fine. Just wanted to try something new for a change. Is there any law says you've got to have coffee and crullers for breakfast every morning of your life?'

'But everybody does.'

'I'm not everybody. I'm me.'

The waitress walked away, mumbling. Buzzy Blake finished the Extra-Cola song, and somebody dropped a dime for Number Two. Fuzzy Fluke, singing about King-Size Tissue. It had a real catchy beat, but Sherry wasn't listening.

'Dick, what's happened?'

I sighed. 'I don't want to talk about it now. It's just that I've made up my mind. I'm sick and tired of being like everybody else on the campus. Wearing the same clothes, eating the same food, listening to the same things, thinking the same thoughts. At least I thought I might experiment a little.'

'Experiment? Look, you better go see your Psych Advisor, I mean it.'

'I'm all right. This is just sort of – well, you might call it a gesture of protest.'

'Protest?' She was really steamed. 'I want you to march right over to the barber shop and get a decent crewcut and then put on some sensible clothes. If you think I'm going to the game with you looking like that this afternoon, you're mistaken.'

'I thought we'd skip the game,' I told her. 'I mean, who cares? Two gangs of apes fighting over a blown-up pig bladder.' Then came the thing that bombed her. 'Besides, we'd have trouble getting there, anyway, I sold my car.'

'*What?*'

'Yesterday. I figured walking's good exercise. As long as I'm right here on the campus all the time, what do I need a car for, anyway?'

'But everybody has a car, even the janitors! Suppose you did want to go to the game, the stadium's half a mile away, how could you walk to—'

She was bombed, all right. Just then somebody put on Number Three, Muzzy Miles and his outfit, and I couldn't hear the end of her sentence. But she was getting up, leaving the booth.

'Hey,' I said, 'what about your breakfast?'

'Never mind, I'm not hungry. And don't bother to get up. I don't want to be seen with you. Now, or ever.'

'But, Sherry—'

She was gone. And Muzzy Miles and a big symphonic chorus did a big production number on Ulcer-Seltzer, with trick camerawork that showed the whole gang singing and dancing inside a set that looked just like your small intestine.

It was just the sort of thing I should have been interested in, because I was sure the Prof would ask questions about it in the next Consumotivation class. But I didn't care about it, or about my meal when it arrived. The poached eggs tasted awful.

So I skipped the cocoa and hurried down the street to the Administration building. I'd lied to Sherry, because I really did plan to see my Psych Advisor.

That was old Hastings, of course, and his office was over three blocks away. It felt kind of funny to walk that far, and I knew a lot of people were hanging out of their car windows and staring at me as I tramped along all alone on the sidewalk.

Halfway there I noticed another guy walking, across the street. It looked like Mark Sawyer, but I couldn't be sure. Mark and I never had anything to say to each other – of course, very few people ever talked to him.

Anyway, that didn't matter. My appointment with old Hastings did.

The girl told me to go right in. Hastings sat there puffing on his pipe and smiling at me. He had the closed-circuit screen on, and I guess he was monitoring some class or other, but when I sat down he turned it off.

'What's the story, Dick?' he asked.

I shrugged. 'No story. Like I said when I called you, I want to change my program to an all-elective course.'

He smiled and puffed. 'You're a senior, aren't you, Dick?'

'You ought to know.' I pointed at the desk. 'You've got my file right there in front of you.'

Old Hastings didn't bat an eyelash. 'Sharp orientation reflex,' he said. 'Bet your father is the same way. He's a pretty big operator up at Major Products, isn't he?'

'President,' I said. 'What's that got to do with it?'

'I wish I knew.' Hastings stopped the nonsense with the pipe and pulled out a regular cigarette with a cancer-canceller filter. 'Look at it my way for a minute. Here's a bright student, doing excellent work for over three years. He tests out perfectly normal all along the line. Excellent adaptability, a conformity-rating of better than ninety-five per cent, routine channelization of all aggressions; a potential company man by any standards. I know, because I've just rechecked your personality profile, semester by semester. So here you are, taking a Junior Exec Course, and doing well. Next year, when you graduate, you'll go right into the Home Office with your father's company. But now you come to me and say you want to drop your studies and switch over to electives. What electives, might I ask?'

'Well, English Lit., for one.'

'You mean Advanced Copywriting?'

'No, English Lit. It's down in my bulletin, under Liberal Arts.'

Hastings chuckled, 'Really, Dick – you must have your old bulletin, from your freshman year. Right? We cut out the whole Liberal Arts Department last semester. Didn't you read about it in the paper? I'm quite sure there was a squib on it somewhere. This is a state university, not a private college. Legislature decided not to appropriate any more funds for frills.'

'What about Philosophy?' I asked.

'Out,' he murmured, and he wasn't smiling, now. 'Don't try and tell me you didn't hear about that. We fired Professor Gotkin the year you came here. A notorious egghead.'

'But I thought – I mean, I hear he's still around. He has a house just off the campus, doesn't he?'

'Unfortunately, there's no way in which the university can compel a man to vacate his own property. But I assure you, Professor Gotkin has absolutely no connection with this institution.'

'Don't some students go up to his place, for some kind of private seminars?'

Hastings ground out his cigarette. 'Let's stop sparring,' he said. 'Have you been seeing Gotkin? Is that where you got these ideas about changing your courses? The truth, now.'

'I'm not on trial.'

'Not yet.'

I gulped. 'Is it a crime to want to study Philosophy?'

'Don't play stupid, Dick. Or course it's no crime, any more than it's a crime to study, say, the history of Russia. Not if the purpose of your study is to get documentation on the evils of Communism. But suppose you didn't have such a sensible, clear-cut purpose and were just reading out of what you believed was idle curiosity? Consciously or unconsciously you'd be laying yourself open to dangerous ideas. Then your study would be a criminal matter. You see that, don't you? Well, the same holds true for Philosophy, or any of those border-line subjects. They're poison, Dick. Poison.'

He stepped over to the window. 'Two hundred million people out there,' he murmured. 'Two hundred million today, and in another generation there'll be three hundred million. Each and every one of them equipped with drives, goals, needs. Each and every one of them vital to our economy as a consumer. All of them dependent upon the skills and techniques of a very few specialists, trained to direct those drives, set up those goals, stimulate and channelize those needs. That's our job here, training the specialists. You're studying to be one of them. Isn't that enough of a positive challenge for you? Why bother with the doubts and illusions of Philosophy?'

'I don't know,' I said. 'And I can't answer until I've investigated.'

Hastings scowled. 'All right you might as well have all of it. I took the liberty of getting in touch with your father this morning, after you called. He told me that under no circumstances should you be permitted to alter your program.'

'I can insist on a hearing. I can take it to the Dean.'

'Please.' He came around the desk and put his hand on my shoulder. 'You know what that would lead to. Now I have another suggestion. It's obvious you've been brooding about this whole business for quite some time. Perhaps you've been subject to pressure from outside influences which you don't care to talk about. That's your affair.

'On the other hand, I'm your Psych Advisor, and your mental health is my affair, too. I recommend an honorable solution. Put in for a two-week leave, for special therapy, and enter the hospital here. Let me handle the treatment. We'll do it with narco-hypnosis. There won't be any conflict involved; when you give us the names of these people – students or faculty members who have been feeding you all this nonsense about rebellion – there'll be no guilt feelings. It's all very open and above-board. And I'm sure it will clear up the whole problem.'

I jerked my shoulder away. I knew his receptionist was listening through the open door, but I didn't care if I shouted.

'All right, to hell with it! You can tell my father whatever you like. Tell him his son is an antisocial egghead for all I care. And as for you, you can take your psychiatric couch and shove it!'

Then I got out.

I went back to my room and waited. Three times the phone rang, and as soon as I recognized my father's voice I hung up.

The fellows came in from classes around noon, and I could hear them going through the hall. None of them stopped at my room. Word must have gone around fast.

Finally, at one o'clock, when most of them were going back to classes, my door opened.

A tall, skinny guy with glasses stood there blinking at me. At first I didn't even recognize him.

'I'm Mark Sawyer,' he said.

'Oh. Come on in, have a chair.'

'I – I heard about this morning.'

'Who hasn't?' I grinned at him. 'Don't tell me you came around to say you're sorry.'

'No. I came around to say I'm glad.' He smiled up at me. 'Surprised, too.'

'Why be surprised?' I shrugged. 'Sooner or later, a guy just gets fed up. You know.'

'Yes, I know. But somehow I never thought you would. None of us did.'

'Us?'

He hesitated. 'Well, you aren't the only one, you know.'

I forced a grin. 'I was beginning to feel that way. When you stop to think, there're over twenty thousand students enrolled here; it gives you sort of a funny feeling when you figure that maybe you're the only one in the whole bunch who doesn't want French fries with his hamburgers.'

'I understand.' He hesitated a minute. 'But are you sure you did not just lose your temper, on impulse?'

'Look, Sawyer. In the past six hours I've lost my girl, got my father sore at me, and told off Hastings. Chances are I'll be expelled before the week is out. Does that sound as if I was acting on impulse?'

'I guess not.' He stood up. 'How'd you like to be my guest this evening? Sort of a bull-session, to meet a couple of other fellows with the same ideas. We usually get together once or twice a week at a friend's house.'

'Well—'

'You might find it interesting. If you feel like it, drop over. Any time after eight. We meet at Professor Gotkin's house.'

He left, then, and the rest of the afternoon passed quietly. But there was a buzzing in my stomach, and when suppertime came I didn't want to eat. I waited until it got dark and then I slipped out and headed for Professor Gotkin's house.

I walked through alleys, wondering if this was the way they always walked: the Commies, the pinkos, the eggheads. It gave me a funny feeling, a feeling of being alone. The game was over now, and the cars were packing the streets; I could hear the horns blaring and the radios going and the guys singing. And I was alone, stumbling through the alley. A dark alley. A blind alley. Alone.

Then I came to the big old house where Professor Gotkin lived, and I wasn't alone any more. Mark Sawyer met me at the door and put out his hand, and he pulled me in, down the hall and through the double doors of the old-fashioned study. I blinked in the sudden glare.

The brightness came from one of those old-fashioned overhead lighting fixtures; come to think of it, I didn't see a single TV lamp in the place, and no TV set, either. Instead, the room was filled with the kind of furniture you wouldn't expect to find anywhere but in a museum. Overstuffed chairs, big sofas, real pre-atomic pieces.

Old Gotkin came up and held out his hand, and he was a museum piece himself. He had long hair, positively bushy, and the oddest glasses I ever saw. They were rimless, so help me.

But what surprised me the most was the guys he introduced me to. There must have been almost a dozen other students in the room, and he took me around and introduced me to them. I don't know what I'd expected, really; I suppose I thought all of them would look something like Mark Sawyer. But he was the only oddball in the whole crowd. All of the other fellows looked perfectly normal and Ivy League, with crewcuts and hornrims. A couple of them even wore army gab pants and Service emblems. There were three girls, too, and I was a little shocked to realize I'd met them all before; two of them were friends of Sherry's, and the third was last year's Junior Prom Queen. Everybody seemed to be acting perfectly natural, and they all smiled at me, but I guess they could tell I was upset.

Professor Gotkin showed me to a big chair – it was a funny-looking thing, no functional lines at all, but it felt kind of comfortable – and then brought me a glass of something that turned out to be beer.

Only it was dark, and tasted strange.

'Glad to have you with us,' he said. 'According to what Mark tells me, you are with us, aren't you?'

Mark Sawyer leaned over my shoulder. 'I hope you don't mind, Dick. I took the liberty of explaining to the gang just what you had to say to me this afternoon.'

I nodded. 'Then I guess there's nothing more to explain.'

'There's one thing you can tell us,' Professor Gotkin murmured. 'What are your plans for the future?'

'Well, I suppose I'd better quit school before they call a hearing and throw me out. After that, I guess I'll have to find a job of my own. My father'll be pretty sore.'

'What sort of a job?'

I thought about it for a moment. 'Factory or manual labor. If I try for anything better, they'll check up on my record here. But maybe that won't be too bad. I mean, it's just five or six hours a day, and I'll have security.'

'Security.' Surprisingly enough, it was the Junior Prom Queen who spoke. 'I thought you were the one who made that remark about not liking French fries with your hamburgers.'

'What's that got to do with it?'

'Everything. Do you know how the average worker lives?'

'Well—'

'Take an ordinary job and you'll be a prisoner for life, in a world of French fries, surrounded by the faceless mob that eats, drinks, dresses, talks and acts on the basis of conditioned reflexes. You'll live in a prefabricated house with a prefabricated wife and a bunch of prefabricated kids. You were taking a Junior Exec course, weren't you? Then you must have studied Depth Motivation Technique. What did you think you were learning that stuff for? In order to use it on consumers against consumers; and who are they? Manual workers, factory workers, the army of conformists and conformity-worshippers you're rebelling against. And now you think you'll find a solution by joining their ranks? Don't be ridiculous!'

'Then what should I do?' I asked.

Professor Gotkin stepped in front of me. 'We've been discussing that, before your arrival,' he said. 'We advise you to stay right here in school.'

'But I can't. I mean, they won't let me change my courses, they told me so.'

He shook his head. 'That's the whole point. You don't change any courses. You make your apologies, take a week off to rest your nerves, and go right back into your studies in Junior Exec.'

For a minute I couldn't believe my ears. 'You mean, keep on doing what I've been doing? And graduate next year, and go into the Corporation, and buy a ranch house, and marry the kind of a girl the Corporation wants me to marry – a girl who'll nag at me until we can buy a bigger ranch house? Be an ex-urbanite, and drive a new car back and forth to work until I keel over with a heart attack and they drive me to the cemetery in a new hearse? Is this your idea of a solution?'

'A necessary step towards a solution,' Mark Sawyer said.

'I don't get it.'

'Listen, what you've just said isn't new. Everybody in this room has sounded off about the same thing, in practically the same words. But all of us are still here, going to school. And all of us will be graduating, taking regular jobs, doing our best to work our way up into key positions. Don't you see that this is the whole secret?'

'Secret of what?'

'The secret of rebellion. The only way a minority can ever hope to win. By infiltration. It's Professor Gotkin's idea.'

He smiled. 'Not original, I assure you. I borrowed it from the Communists.'

'But – you are a Communist, aren't you?' I asked.

He frowned. 'Not at all. A Communist, actually, is the follower of a political doctrine, a believer in community property, who seeks to overthrow other governmental systems by force, if necessary.'

'That isn't the way I heard it.'

His frown deepened. 'That's right, I'd forgotten. They don't teach that definition any more, do they? To you, a Communist is anyone whose ideas differ from those of the majority – or, rather, from the ideas superimposed upon the majority, who accept them without thinking. A Communist is an egghead is an individualist is a psychotic; isn't that how it goes?'

'Something like that, yes.'

'And you think that any expression of nonconformity, and difference of taste from that of the mathematical majority, is an automatic indication of a maladjusted personality?'

'I suppose so.'

'Still, you are aware of such a difference in yourself?' His frown smoothed into a smile. 'Don't bother to answer that, Dick. Because we all feel the same way. Only we've learned not to be ashamed of it. We know that the history of this nation is a history of constant rebellion. It was political rebellion which won our freedom, social rebellion which expanded our frontiers, intellectual rebellion which resulted in invention and progress. Only in recent years have we fallen into the error of orientating our philosophy around an expanding economy, dependent upon a constant and complacent consumerdom. Only in recent years has it come to be a shameful thing to be "different" – and individuality is equated with antisocial attitudes.

'I know, because I've lived through the change. The get-in-line-and-stay-in-line doctrine was imposed as a necessity during the War, and somehow we never managed to abandon it after the shooting was over. Mass media dedicated itself to the noble purpose of selling masses of goods to the mass audience. From that, it was only a step to the mass merchandizing of ideas. Then came the real Communist scare; we began to be afraid of eggheads – and everybody who criticized was given that label. It's still a label, today, but soon it may be down on the books as a legal synonym for traitor. Unless we take decisive steps to prevent it.'

'But what good will my returning to school do? How will it be helping to rebel by staying in line?'

'Through infiltration,' the Professor said. 'Don't you see? We're all doing it. Granted, the process is a slow one, but it will bear fruit. If, within ten years or even twenty years, every student in this room will have attained a position of importance in the outside world, there will be a chance to reverse the trend. A legislator here, a banker there, a business executive, an advertising magnate, a newspaper man, a TV producer – people like that are in a position to influence key decisions from the top level.'

I glanced around. 'There's only eleven of us,' I said. 'A drop in the bucket.'

Mark Sawyer cleared his throat. 'You'd be surprised if you knew how many there really were,' he told me. 'Not everybody's here tonight. I'll bet we have almost fifty on the campus.'

'Fifty out of twenty-three thousand students?'

'Fifty of the best. The individualists, the clear-headed ones. And this isn't the only campus in the country, remember.' Professor Gotkin drew himself up. 'Since I left – since I was fired, rather – I haven't been idle. My connections with colleagues all over the nation have served me well. There are groups like these scattered throughout the schools, and in other places where you'd least suspect it. Army camps, labor unions, fraternal organizations; yes, and the very strongholds of the status quo. Most of our followers are young men and women like yourself, yes, and it is from their ranks that we'll draw our real strength in the future. But even now we've got a slight toe-hold in high places. Would it surprise you if I revealed that we've already enlisted several important educators in our ranks? And no less than six Congressmen? And two practicing "industrial psychologists" who specialize in Depth Motivation techniques?' He chuckled. 'We're not entirely impractical, you see. Nor entirely helpless. But there's much to be done, and we can use able assistance. We need men like you, Dick. What do you say?'

I hesitated. 'How can I be sure that you're telling me the truth?'

'A sensible reaction. And one I'll be glad to honor. It so happens that there are lists available to me. You are welcome to inspect the names of your – shall we call them fellow-egg-heads? – right here in school. As the situation warrants, I'll acquaint you with other members of the movement in the outside world; we hope to be eventually forming little key groups in selected industries and professions in time to come.'

'You aren't going to start a revolution? You're sure of it?'

'Of course we are! But not an armed revolution; we don't intend to overthrow the government by violence. Ours will be a much more far-reaching and long-lasting rebellion. A revolution of ideas. We're going to take the world away from the pitchmen and their puppets and give it back to the individual, the free citizen. Are you with us?'

I nodded.

'What do you want me to do?' I asked. 'Where do I begin?'

'You begin by going back to your Psych Advisor. Apologize to him. Tell him you had a fight with your girl, tell him you've been under a strain. If he suggests rest or treatment, take it. But no narco-hypnosis, of course. You understand why.'

I nodded.

'Then, return to your classes. I'm sure there'll be no real difficulty. You have a brilliant record. Your father and your girl will come around. Just carry on as you did before this happened.'

I stood up. 'But don't I do anything? I mean, aren't you carrying out any kind of program at all here on the campus?'

'You mean some sort of underground protest movement or sabotage?' Professor Gotkin shook his head. 'We aren't ready for that yet. In a few years, perhaps, when our group is stronger. Meanwhile, about all we do is proselyte. And that's where someone like yourself will come in handy. Maybe we can work out a system, a way of bringing in more potential recruits. It's worth thinking about and planning for.'

'Will there be meetings like this regularly?'

'Yes, but not according to any schedule. We can't afford to attract too much attention at this stage of the game. And another thing; we don't believe it wise to congregate in social groups or be seen together anywhere outside this house. The notice of the next meeting will come to you from one of your fellow members. I suggest, therefore, that you take steps to memorize their names.'

'An excellent idea.' I made a circuit of the room slowly, shaking hands with each of my fellow conspirators. As I did so, I asked each one to repeat his or her name to me.

'Don't forget, now,' Professor Gotkin cautioned.

'I won't.'

'You'll be notified when to come again.'

'I'll be here.'

And, about a week later, I was. A lot happened in the meantime. I'd seen old Hastings and the Dean. I saw my father, too, and then there was a special two-day trip which nobody knew about. That is, not until I walked into the next meeting at Professor Gotkin's house, with the Security officers right behind me.

We caught fifteen of the lousy eggheads right then and there, and of course we got hold of the old buzzard's secret lists.

Every last one of the subversive rats on the campus was rounded up, and I was surprised at some of the big wheels who were in on the plot.

But it was like that all over the country, they tell me. And it made a real stink – I guess you must have read about it in the papers, though.

Of course, I don't claim credit for the whole thing. It was Dad's idea in the first place, when he got wind of some kind of Commie activity down here at the school. He even supplied me with the little portable wire-recorder I'd hidden in my coat when I went to Gotkin's house the first time; and that clinched it. No matter what he and the others said, they couldn't deny the evidence – it was all down on tape, the whole subversive pitch, even their names in their own voices.

Right now I guess they're being held on open charges, but that's just a formality. Dad is in pretty thick with all the right people, and they say that in just a couple of weeks Congress is going to pass a Treason Law to take care of the whole gang. It'll be retroactive, of course. They're even talking about something called the Egghead Amendment to the Constitution.

Naturally, I'm pretty happy about the way things worked out. It wasn't much fun having to pretend to be psycho, even for a little while – it must be awful to actually be that way, all queer and alone.

But it's all over now, and I'm back at school, and Sherry's with me, and Dad bought me a new convertible, and I guess right now you might say I'm kind of a hero.

It wouldn't surprise me a bit if I was elected president of the Class of 1978.

DEAD-END DOCTOR

THE last psychiatrist on Earth sat alone in a room. There was a knock on the door.

'Come in,' he said.

A tall robot entered, the electronic beam of its single eye piercing the gloom and focusing on the psychiatrist's face.

'Dr. Anson,' the robot said, 'the rent is due today. Pay me.'

Dr. Howard Anson blinked. He did not like the harsh light, nor the harsh voice, nor the harsh meaning of the message. As he rose, he attempted to conceal his inner reactions with a bland smile, then remembered that his facial expression meant nothing to the robot.

That was precisely the trouble with the damned things, he told himself, you couldn't use psychology on them.

'Sixty tokens,' the robot chanted, and rolled across the room toward him.

'But—' Dr. Anson hesitated, then took the plunge. 'But I haven't got sixty tokens at the moment. I told the manager yesterday. If you'll only give me a little time, a slight extension of credit—'

'Sixty tokens,' the robot repeated, as if totally unmindful of the interruption, which, Dr. Anson assured himself, was exactly the case. The robot was unmindful. It did not react to unpredictable factors; that was not its function. The robot didn't see the rental figures in this office building and had no power to make decisions, regarding credit. It was built to collect the rent, nothing more.

But that was enough. More than enough.

The robot rolled closer. Its arms rose and the hook-like terminals slid back the panels in its chest to reveal a row of push buttons and a thin, narrow slot.

'The rent is due,' repeated the robot. 'Please deposit the tokens in the slot.'

Anson sighed. 'Very well,' he said. He walked over to his desk, opened a drawer and scooped out half a dozen shiny disks.

He slipped the disks into the slot. They landed inside the robot's cylindrical belly with a series of dull plops. Evidently the robot had been making the rounds of the building all day; it sounded more than half full.

For a wild moment, Dr. Anson wondered what would happen if he kidnapped the robot and emptied its cashbox. His own medical specialty was psychiatry and neurosurgery, and he was none too certain of a robot's anatomical structure, but he felt sure he could fool around until he located the jackpot. He visualized himself standing before the operating table, under the bright lights. 'Scalpel – forceps – blow-torch—'

But that was unthinkable. Nobody had ever dared to rob a robot. Nobody ever robbed anything or anyone today, which was part of the reason Dr. Anson couldn't pay his rent on time.

Still, he had paid it. The robot's terminals were punching push buttons in its chest and now its mouth opened. 'Here is your receipt,' it said and a pink slip slid out from its mouth like a paper tongue.

Anson accepted the slip and the mouth said, 'Thank you.'

The terminals closed the chest-panels, the electronic beam swept the corners as the wheels turned, and the robot rolled out of the room and down the corridor.

Anson closed the door and mopped his brow.

So far, so good. But what would happen when the robot reached the manager? He'd open his walking cash register and discover Anson's six ten-token disks. Being human, he'd recognize them for what they were – counterfeit.

Dr. Anson shuddered. To think that it had come to this, a reputable psychiatrist committing a crime!

He considered the irony. In a world totally devoid of anti-social activity, there were no antisocial tendencies which required the services of psychiatry. And that was why he, as the last living psychiatrist, had to resort to antisocial activity in order to survive.

Probably it was only his knowledge of antisocial behavior, in the abstract, which enabled him to depart from the norm and indulge in such actions in the concrete.

Well, he was in the concrete now and it would harden fast – unless something happened. At best, his deception would give him a few days' grace. After that, he could face only disgrace.

Anson shook his head and sat down behind the desk. Maybe this was the beginning he told himself. First counterfeiting and fraud, then robbery and embezzlement, then rape and murder. Who could say where it would all end?

'Physician, heal thyself,' he murmured and glanced with distaste at the dust-covered couch, where no patient reposed; where, indeed, no patient had ever reposed since he'd opened his office almost a year ago.

It had been a mistake, he realized. A big mistake ever to listen to his father and—

The visio lit up and the audio hummed. Anson turned and confronted a gigantic face. The gigantic face let out a gigantic roar, almost shattering the screen.

'I'm on my way up, Doctor!' the face bellowed. 'Don't try to sneak out! I'm going to break your neck with my bare hands!'

For a few seconds Anson sat there in his chair, too numb to move. Then the full import of what he had seen and heard reached him. The manager was coming to kill him!

'Hooray!' he said under his breath and smiled. It was almost too good to be true. After all this time, at last, somebody was breaking loose. A badly disturbed personality, a potential killer, was on his way up – he was finally going to get himself a patient. If he could treat him before being murdered, that is.

Tingling with excitement, Anson fumbled around in his

files. Now where in thunder was that equipment for the Rorschach test? Yes, and the Porteus Maze and—

The manager strode into the room without knocking. Anson looked up, ready to counter the first blast of aggression with a steely professional stare.

But the manager was smiling.

'Sorry I blew up that way,' he said. 'Guess I owe you an apology.'

'When I found those counterfeit tokens, something just seemed to snap for a moment,' the manager explained. 'You know how it is.'

'Yes, I do,' said Anson eagerly. 'I understand quite well. And it's nothing to be ashamed of. I'm sure that with your co-operation, we can get to the roots of the trauma. Now if you'll just relax on the couch over there—'

The red-faced little man continued to smile, but his voice was brusque. 'Nonsense! I don't need any of that. Before I came up here, I stopped in at Dr. Peabody's office, down on the sixth floor. Great little endocrinologist, that guy. Gave me some kind of shot that fixed me up in a trice. That's three times faster than a jiffy, you know.'

'I don't know,' Anson answered vaguely. 'Endocrinology isn't my field.'

'Well, it should be. It's the only field in medicine that really amounts to anything nowadays. Except for diagnosis and surgery, of course. Those gland-handers can do anything. Shots for when you feel depressed, shots for when you're afraid, shots for when you get excited, or mad, the way I was. Boy, I feel great now. At peace with the world!'

'But it won't last. Sooner or later, you'll get angry again.'

'So I'll get another shot,' the manager replied. 'Everybody does.'

'That's not a solution. You're merely treating the symptom, not the basic cause.' Anson rose and stepped forward. 'You're under a great deal of tension. I suspect it goes back to early childhood. Did you suffer from enuresis?'

'It's my turn to ask questions. What about those fake tokens you tried to palm off on me?'

'Why, it was all a joke. I thought if you could give me a few more days to dig up—'

'I'm giving you just five minutes to dig down,' the manager said, smiling pleasantly, but firmly. 'You ought to know that you can't pull a trick like that with a cash collector; these new models have automatic tabulators and detectors. The moment that robot came back to my office, it spat up the counterfeits. It couldn't stomach them. And neither can I.'

'Stomach?' asked Anson hopefully. 'Are you ever troubled with gastric disturbances? Ulcers? Psychosomatic pain in the—'

The manager thrust out his jaw. 'Look here, Anson, you're not a bad sort, really. It's just that you're confused. Why don't you clever up and look at the big picture? This witch-doctor racket of yours, it's atomized. Nobody's got any use for it today. You're like the guys who used to manufacture buggy whips; they sat around telling themselves that the automobile would never replace the horse, when any street-cleaner could see what was happening to business.

'Why don't you admit you're licked? The gland-handers have taken over. Why, a man would have to be crazy to go to a psychiatrist nowadays and you know there aren't any crazy people any more. So forget about all this. Take a course or something. You can be an End-Doc yourself. Then open up a real office and make yourself some big tokens.'

Anson shook his head. 'Sorry,' he said. 'Not interested.'

The manager spread his hands. 'All right. I gave you a chance. Now there's nothing left to do but call in the ejectors.'

He walked over and opened the door. Apparently he had been prepared for Anson's decision, because two ejectors were waiting. They rolled into the room and, without bothering to focus their beams on Anson, commenced to scoop books from the shelves and deposit them in their big open belly-hampers.

'Wait!' Anson cried, but the ejector robots continued inexorably and alphabetically: there went Adler, Brill, Carmichael, Dunbar, Ellis, Freud, Gresell, Horney, Isaacs, Jung, Kardiner, Lindner, Moll—

'Darling, what's the matter?'

Sue Porter was in the room. Then she was in his arms and Dr. Anson had a difficult time remembering what the matter was. The girl affected him that way.

But a look at the manager's drugged smile served as a reminder. Anson's face reddened, due to a combination of embarrassment and lipstick smudges, as he told Sue what had happened.

Sue laughed. 'Well, if that's all it is, what are you so upset about?' Without waiting for a reply, she advanced upon the manager, her hand digging into her middle bra-cup. 'Here's your tokens,' she said. 'Now call off the ejectors.'

The manager accepted the disks with a smile of pure euphoria, then strode over to the robots and punched buttons. The ejectors halted their labors between Reich and Stekel, then reversed operations. Quickly and efficiently, they replaced all the books on the shelves.

In less than a minute. Anson faced the girl in privacy. 'You shouldn't have done that,' he said severely.

'But, darling, I wanted to. After all, what are a few tokens more or less?'

'A few tokens?' Anson scowled. 'In the past year, I've borrowed over two thousand from you. This can't go on.'

'Of course not,' the girl agreed. 'That's what I've been telling you. Let's get a Permanent and then Daddy will give you a nice fat job and—'

'There you go again! How often must I warn you about the Elektra situation? This unnatural dependency on the father image is dangerous. If only you'd let me get you down on the couch—'

'Why, of course, darling!'

'No, no!' Anson cried. 'I want to analyze you!'

128

'Not now,' Sue answered. 'We'll be late for dinner. Daddy expects you.'

'Damn dinner and damn Daddy, too,' Anson said. But he took the girl's arm and left the office, contenting himself by slamming the door.

'Aren't you going to put up that "Doctor Will Return in Two Hours" sign?' the girl asked, glancing back at the door.

'No,' Anson told her. 'I'm not coming back in two hours. Or ever.'

Sue gave him a puzzled look, but her eyes were smiling.

Dr. Howard Anson's eyes weren't smiling as he and Sue took off from the roof. He kept them closed, so that he didn't have to watch the launching robots, or note the 'copter's progress as it soared above the city. He didn't want to gaze down at the metallic tangle of conveyors moving between the factories or the stiffly striding figures which supervised their progress on the ramps and loading platforms. The air about them was filled with 'copters, homeward bound from offices and recreation areas, but no human figures moved in the streets. Ground level was almost entirely mechanized.

'What's the matter now?' Sue's voice made him look at her. Her eyes held genuine concern.

'The sins of the fathers,' Anson said. 'Yours and mine.' He watched the girl as she set the 'copter on auto-pilot for the journey across the river. 'Of course it really wasn't my father's fault that he steered me into psychiatry. After all, it's been a family tradition for a hundred and fifty years. All my paternal ancestors were psychiatrists, with the exception of one or two renegade Behaviorists. When he encouraged my interest in the profession, I never stopped to question him. He trained me – and I was the last student to take up the specialty at medical school. The last, mind you!

'I should have known then that it was useless. But he kept insisting this state of affairs couldn't last, that things were sure to change. "Cheer up," he used to tell me, whenever I got discouraged. "The pendulum is bound to swing in the other direction." And then he'd tell me about the good old days when he was a boy and the world was still full of fetishism, and hebephrenia and pyromania and mixoscopic zoophilia. "It will come again," he kept telling me. "Just you wait and see! We'll have frottage and nympholepsy and compulsive exhibitionism – everything your little heart desires."

'Well, he was wrong. He died knowing that he had set me up in a dead-end profession. I'm an anachronism, like the factory worker or the farmer or the miner or the soldier. We don't have any need for them in our society any more; robots have replaced them all. And the End-Docs have replaced the psychiatrists and neuro-surgeons. With robots to ease the physical and economic burden and gland-handers to relieve mental tension, there's nothing left for me. The last psychiatrist should have disappeared along with the last advertising man. Come to think of it, they probably belong together. My father was wrong, Sue, I know that now. But most of the real blame belongs to your father.'

'Daddy?' she exclaimed. 'How can you possibly blame him?'

Anson laughed shortly. 'Your family has been pioneering in robotics almost as long as mine has worked in psychiatry. One of your ancestors took out the first basic patent. If it weren't for him and those endocrine shots, everything would still be normal – lots of incest and scoptophilia, plenty of voyeurism for everybody—'

'Why, darling, what a thing to say! You know as well as I do what robots have done for the world. You said it yourself. We don't have any more manual or menial labor. There's no war, plenty of everything for everybody. And Daddy isn't stopping there.'

'I suppose not,' Anson said bitterly. 'What is the old devil dreaming up now?'

Sue flushed. 'You wouldn't talk like that if you knew just how hard he's been working. He and Mr. Mullet, the engineering chief. They're just about ready to bring out the new pilot models they've developed for space travel.'

'I've heard that one before. They've been announcing those models for ten years.'

'They keep running into bugs. I guess. But sooner or later, they'll find a way to handle things. Nothing is perfect, you know. Every once in a while, there's still some trouble with the more complicated models.'

'But they keep trying for perfection. Don't you see where all this leads to, Sue? Human beings will become obsolescent. First the workers, now the psychiatrists and other professions. But it won't end there. Inside of another generation or two, we won't need anyone any more. Your father, or somebody like him, will produce the ultimate robot – the robot that's capable of building other robots and directing them. Come to think of it, he's already done the first job; your factories are self-perpetuating. All we need now is a robot that can take the place of a few key figures like your father. Then that's the end of the human race. Oh, maybe they'll keep a few men and women around for pets, but that's all. And thank God I won't be here to see it.'

'So why worry?' Sue replied. 'Enjoy yourself while you can. We'll apply for a Permanent and Daddy will give you a job like he promised me—'

'Job? What kind of job?'

'Oh, maybe he'll make you a vice-president or something. They don't have to do anything.'

'Fine! A wonderful future!'

'I don't see anything wrong with it. You ought to consider yourself lucky.'

'Listen, Sue.' He turned to her earnestly. 'You just don't understand the way I feel. I've spent eighteen years of my life in school, six of it in training for my profession. That's all I know and I know it well. And what have I to show for it? I'm a psychiatrist who's never had a patient, a neuro-surgeon who's never performed anything but an experimental topectomy or lobotomy. That's my work, my life, and I want a chance to function. I don't intend to sit around on a fat sinecure, raising children whose only future is oblivion. I don't want a Permanent with you under those conditions.'

She sniffed petulantly. 'A Permanent with me isn't good enough, is that it? I suppose you'd rather have a lot of repression and guilt complexes and all that other stuff you're always talking about.'

'It isn't that,' Anson insisted. 'I don't really want the world to revert to neurotic or psychotic behavior just so I can have a practice. But damn it, I can't stand to see the way things are going. We've done away with stress and privation and tension and superstition and intolerance, and that's great. But we've also done away with ourselves in the process. We're getting to the point where we, as human beings, no longer have a function to perform. We're not needed.'

The girl gave him an angry glance. 'What you're trying to say is that you don't need me, is that it?'

'I do need you. But not on these terms. I'm not going to lead a useless existence, or bring children into a world where they'll be useless. And if your father brings up that vice-president deal at dinner tonight, I'm going to tell him to take his job and—'

'Never mind!' Sue flipped the switch from auto-pilot back to manual and the 'copter turned. 'You needn't bother about dinner. I'll take you back to your office now. You can put yourself down on the couch and do a little practicing on your own mind. You need it! Of all the stupid, pig-headed—'

The sound of the crash reached them even at flying level. Sue Porter broke off abruptly and glanced down at the river front below. Anson stared with her.

'What was that?' he asked.

'I don't know – can't make it out from here.' She spun the controls, guiding the 'copter down until it hovered over the scene of accelerating confusion.

A huge loading barge was moored against one of the docks. Had been moored, rather; as they watched, it swung erratically into the current, then banged back against the pier. Huge piles of machinery, only partially lashed to the deck, now tumbled and broke free. Some of the cranes splashed into the water and others rolled across the flat surface of the barge.

'Accident,' Sue gasped. 'The cable must have broken.'

Anson's eyes focused on the metallic figures which dotted the deck and stood stolidly on the dock. 'Look at the robots!'

'What about them?' asked Sue.

'Aren't they supposed to be doing something? That one with the antenna – isn't it designed to send out a warning signal when something goes wrong?'

'You're right. They beam Emergency in a case like this. The expediters should be out by now.'

'Some of them look as if they're paralyzed,' Anson noted, observing a half-dozen of the metallic figures aboard the barge. They were rigid, unmoving. Even as he watched, a round steel bell bowled across the deck. None of the robots moved – the sphere struck them like a ball hitting the pins and hurtled them into the water.

On the pier, the immobilized watchers gave no indication of reaction.

'Paralyzed,' Anson repeated.

'Not that one!'

Sue pointed excitedly as the 'copter hovered over the deck. Anson looked and found the cause of her consternation.

A large, fully articulated robot with the humanoid face of a controller clattered along in a silvery blur of motion. From one of its four upper appendages dangled a broad-bladed axe.

It bumped squarely against an armless receptacle-type robot in its loading compartment. There was a crash as the victim collapsed.

And the controller robot sped on, striking at random, in a series of sped-up motions almost impossible to follow – but not impossible to understand.

'That's the answer!' said Anson. 'It must have cut the cable with the axe. And attacked the others, to immobilize them. Come on, let's land this thing.'

'But we can't go down there! It's dangerous! Somebody will send out the alarm. The expediters will handle it—'

'Land!' Anson commanded. He began to rummage around in the rear compartment of the 'copter.

'What are you looking for?' Sue asked as she maneuvered the machine to a clear space alongside a shed next to the dock.

'The rope ladder.'

'But we won't need it. We're on the ground.'

'I need it.' He produced the tangled length and began to uncoil it. 'You stay here,' he said. 'This is my job.'

'What are you going to do?'

'Yes, what are you going to do?' The deep voice came from the side of the 'copter. Anson and Sue looked up at the face of Eldon Porter.

'Daddy! How did you get here?'

'Alarm came through.'

The big, gray-haired man scowled at the dock beyond where the expediter robots were already mopping up with flame-throwers.

'You've got no business here,' Eldon Porter said harshly. 'This area's off limits until everything's under control.' He turned to Anson. 'And I'll have to ask you to forget everything you've seen here. We don't want word of accidents like these to leak out – just get people needlessly upset.'

'Then this isn't the first time?' asked Anson.

'Of course not. Mullet's had a lot of experience; he knows how to handle this.'

'Right, Chief.' Anson recognized the thin, bespectacled engineer at Eldon's Porter's side. 'Every time we test out one of these advanced models, something goes haywire. Shock, overload, some damned thing. Only thing we can do is scrap it and try again. So you folks keep out of the way. We're going to corner it with the flame-throwers and—'

'No!'

Anson opened the door and climbed out, dragging the long rope ladder behind him.

'Where in hell do you think you're going?' demanded Eldon Porter.

'I'm after that robot,' Anson said. 'Give me two of your men to hold the ends of this ladder. We can use it like a net and capture the thing without destroying it. That is, put it in restraint.'

'Restraint?'

'Technical term we psychiatrists use.' Anson smiled at the two men and then at the girl. 'Don't worry,' he said. 'I know what I'm doing. I've got a case at last. Your robot is psychotic.'

'Psychotic,' grumbled Eldon Porter, watching the young man move away. 'What's that mean?'

'Nuts,' said Sue sweetly. 'A technical term.'

Several weeks passed before Sue saw Dr. Howard Anson again.

She waited anxiously outside in the corridor with her father until the young man emerged. He peeled off his gloves, smiling.

'Well?' rumbled Eldon Porter.

'Ask Mullet,' Anson suggested.

'He did it!' the thin engineer exulted. 'It works, just like he said it would! Now we can use the technique whenever there's a breakdown. But I don't think we'll have any more. Not if we incorporate his suggestions in the new designs. We can use them on the new space pilot models, too.'

'Wonderful!' Eldon Porter said. He put his hand on Anson's shoulder. 'We owe you a lot.'

'Mullet deserves the credit,' Anson replied. 'If not for him and his schematics, I'd never have made it. He worked with me night and day, feeding me the information. We correlated everything – you know, I'd never realized how closely your engineers had followed the human motor-reaction patterns.'

Eldon Porter cleared his throat. 'About that job,' he began. 'That vice-presidency—'

'Of course,' Anson said. 'I'll take it. There's going to be a lot of work to do. I want to train at least a dozen men to handle emergencies until the new models take over. I understand you've had plenty of cases like this in the past.'

'Right. And we've always ended up by junking the robots that went haywire. Hushed it up, of course, so people wouldn't worry. Now we're all set. We can duplicate the electronic patterns of the human brain without worrying about breakdowns due to speed-up or overload. Why didn't we think of the psychiatric approach ourselves?'

'Leave that to me,' Anson said. And as the two men moved off, he made a psychiatric approach toward the girl.

She finally stepped back out of his arms. 'You owe me an explanation. What's the big idea? You're taking the job, after all!'

'I've found I can be useful,' Anson told her. 'There is a place for my profession – a big one. Human beings no longer go berserk, but robots do.'

'Is that what this is all about? Have you been psycho-analyzing the robot you caught?'

Anson smiled. 'I'm afraid psychoanalysis isn't suitable for robots. The trouble is purely mechanical. But the brain is a mechanism, too. The more I worked with Mullet, the more I learned about the similarities.'

'You cured that robot in there?' she asked incredulously.

'That's right.' Anson slipped out of his white gown. 'It's as good as new, ready to go back on the job at once. Of course it will have slower, less intense reactions, but its judgment hasn't been impaired. Neuro-surgery did the trick. That's the answer, Sue. Once you open them up, you can see the cure's the same.'

'So that's why you were wearing a surgical gown,' she said. 'You were operating on the robot.'

Anson grinned triumphantly. 'The robot was excited, in a

state of hysteria. I merely applied my knowledge and skill to the problem.'

'But what kind of an operation?'

'I opened up the skull and eased the pressure on the overload wires. There used to be a name for it, but now there's a new one.' Anson took her back into his arms. 'Darling, congratulate me! I've just successfully performed the first prefrontal robotomy!'

CHANGE OF HEART

It had been the sun, the moon, the stars to me – a whirling planet of silver, held to its orbit by a glittering chain. Uncle Hansi would twirl it before my eyes on those long, faraway Sunday afternoons. Sometimes he let me press the icy surface against my ear, and then I heard from deep within it the music of the spheres.

Now it was only a battered old watch, a keepsake inheritance. The once gleaming case was worn and dented, and a deep scratch crossed the finely etched initials below the stem.

I took it to a jeweller's on the Avenue, for an estimate, and the clerk was frigidly polite. 'We've hardly the facilities to handle such repair work here. Perhaps some small shop, a watchmaker of the old school—'

He laid it carelessly on the counter, for he did not know that this was a dying planet, a waning world, a star that flamed in first magnitude in the bygone eons of my childhood.

So I put the world in my pocket and went away from there. I walked home through the Village and came, eventually, to the establishment of Ulrich Klemm.

The basement window was grimy with the dust of years, and the gold lettering had flecked and moted, but the name caught my eye. 'ULRICH KLEMM, WATCHMAKER.'

I descended five steps, turned the doorknob, and walked into a seething symphony of sound. Whispers, murmurs, frantic titterings. Deep buzzings and shrill cadences. Muted, measured, mechanical rhythms, set in eternal order – the testament of Time.

Against shadowed walls the faces loomed and leered. They

were big, they were small, they were round or oval or broad; high and low they hung, these clock-faces in the shop of Ulrich Klemm, ticking and staring at me in darkness.

The white head of the watchmaker was haloed in the light of his workbench. He turned and rose, then shuffled over to the counter, his padding feet weaving in counter-point to the rhythms of the clockwork on the walls.

'There iss something?' he asked. I stared into his face – the face of a grandfather's clock; weathered, patient, enduring, inscrutable.

'I want you to have a look at this,' I said. 'My Uncle Hansi willed it to me, but the regular jewellers don't seem to know how to put it in working order.'

As I put Uncle Hansi's watch on the counter, the face of the grandfather's clock leaned forward. All of the faces on the wall gazed and gaped while I explained.

Ulrich Klemm nodded. His gnarled hands (do all grandfather's clocks have gnarled hands? I wondered) carried the battered old timepiece over to the light above the workbench.

I watched the hands. They did not tremble. The fingers suddenly became instruments. They opened, revealed, pried, probed, delicately dissected.

'Yess. I can repair this, I think.' He spoke to me, to all the faces on the wall.

'It will not be easy. These parts – they are no longer made. I shall have to fashion them especially. But it iss a fine watch, yess, and worth the effort.'

I opened my mouth, but did not speak. The faces on the wall spoke for me.

For suddenly the sound surged to a crescendo, sharp and shrill. The faces laughed and gurgled and shrieked; a hundred voices, accents, tongues and intonations met and mingled. Six times the voices rose and fell proclaiming—

'It's six o'clock, Grandfather.'

No, it wasn't my imagination. The voice said that. Not the mechanical voice, but the other one. The one that came from the long, slim, incredibly white throat of the girl who emerged from the rear of the shop.

'Yess, Lisa?' The old man cocked his head.

'Dinner is ready. Oh, excuse me – I thought you were alone.' I stared at golden hair and silver flesh. Lisa. The granddaughter. The clocks ticked on, and something leapt in rhythm deep in my chest.

She smiled. I smiled. Ulrich introduced her. And I became crafty, persuasive. I leaned over the counter and artfully led the conversation along, encouraging him to talk of the marvels of clockwork, of old days in Switzerland when Ulrich Klemm was a horologist of renown.

It wasn't difficult. He extended an invitation to share the meal, and soon I was in one of the rooms behind the shop, listening to further reminiscences.

He spoke of the golden days of clockwork, of automata – mechanical chessplayers, birds that sang and flew, soldiers walking and sounding trumpets, angels in belfries chorusing the coming of day and brandishing swords against Evil.

Ulrich Klemm showed me the picture on his wall – the picture he had salvaged years ago when he and Lisa fled from Europe to the refuge of this tiny shop in the Village. The picture was a landscape, with railroad tracks running through a mountain pass. He wound a spring at the side of the frame and the train came out and raced through a tunnel, climbed the grade and disappeared again. It was a marvelous picture, and I told him so.

But no picture, however animated, could satisfy me as did the sight of Lisa. And while my tongue responded to the old man, my eyes answered the girl.

We didn't say much to one another. She cut her finger while serving the meat, and I bandaged it as the blood flowed. We spoke of the weather, of trivial things. But when I departed I had wrung an invitation to come again from Ulrich Klemm. Lisa smiled and nodded as I left, and she smiled and nodded again that night in my dreams.

So it was that I came often to the little shop, even after my watch had been repaired and restored to me. Ulrich Klemm enjoyed an audience – he dreamed and boasted before me for long hours. He told me of things he had created in the old country; of royal commissions, mechanical marvels, medals and awards.

'There iss nothing I cannot fathom once I turn my hand to it,' he often said. 'All Nature – just a mechanism. When I wass a young man, my father wished for me to become a surgeon. But the human body iss a poor instrument, full of flaws. A good chronometer, that iss perfection.'

I listened and nodded and waited. And in time, I achieved my goal.

Lisa and I became friends, bit by bit. We smiled, we spoke, we went walking together. We went to the park, to the theater.

It was simple, once the initial barriers were surmounted. For Lisa had no friends, and her school days were an alien memory. Ulrich Klemm treasured her with morbid jealousy. She and she alone had never failed him; she responded perfectly to his will. That is what the old man desired – he loved automatons.

But I loved Lisa. Lisa the girl, Lisa the woman. I dreamed of an awakening, an emergence into the world beyond the four walls of the shop. And in time I spoke to her of what I planned.

'No, Dane,' she said. 'He will never let me go. He is old and all alone. If we can wait, in a few years—'

'Wake up,' I said. 'This is New York, the twentieth century. You're of age. And I want you to marry me. Now.'

'No,' she sighed. 'We cannot do this to him.' And shook her head, like an automaton.

It was like something out of the Dark Ages. It was a world apart from my office uptown, with its talk of surveys and projects and a branch managership opening for me in Detroit.

I told her about the Detroit assignment. I insisted on speaking now. Lisa wept then, and Lisa pleaded, but in the end I went to the old man and told him.

'I'm going to marry Lisa,' I said. 'I'm going to take her with me. Now.'

'No-no-no-no,' ticked the clocks on the wall. 'NO – NO – NO,' boomed the chimes. And, 'You cannot take her!' shouted Ulrich Klemm. 'She iss all I have left. No one will ever take her from me. Never.'

It was useless to argue. And when I pleaded with Lisa to elope, to run away, she turned the blank perfection of a clock-face towards me and ticked, 'No.' For Lisa was the old man's masterpiece. He had spent years perfecting her pattern of obedient reaction. I saw that I could never tamper with Ulrich Klemm's delicate adjustments.

So I went away, carrying my silver watch on a chain in my pocket; knowing that I could never find a chain that would link Lisa to me. During the months in Detroit I wrote frequently to the shop, but there was no answer.

I instructed a friend of mine to stop by and deliver messages, but I heard no word. The silver watch in my pocket ticked off the days and the weeks and the months, and finally I returned to New York.

Then I heard that Lisa was dead.

My friend had stopped by and found the shop shuttered and deserted. Going around to the rear, he roused Ulrich Klemm from his vigil. The haggard, sleepless old man said that Lisa had suffered a heart attack. She was dying.

Returning several days later, my friend was unable to rouse anyone. But the wreath on the door of the locked shop told its own grim story.

I thanked my informant, sighed, nodded, and went out into the wintry streets.

It was a bitterly cold day. My breath plumed before me, and I stamped the snow from my shoes as I descended the steps to Ulrich Klemm's door. The glass was frosted like a wedding cake; I could not see into the shop through the sheet of ice.

My gloved hand tugged the doorknob. The door rattled, but

did not open. I knocked. The old man was a little deaf, yet he must hear, he must answer. I knocked again.

Quite suddenly the door opened. I stepped over the threshold, into a vacuum of darkness and silence. No light shone over the workbench, no chimes heralded my entrance. And the clock-faces were invisible, inaudible. The absence of the familiar ticking struck me like a physical blow. It was as though a world had ended.

Everything had stopped. And yet Ulrich Klemm's crazed fanaticism would not permit a stopping, an ending—

'Klemm,' I said. 'Turn on the lights. It's Dane.'

Then I heard the voice, the soft voice murmuring up at me. 'You've come back. Oh, I knew you would come back.'

'Lisa!'

'Yes, dearest. I have been waiting for you here, all alone. So long it has been, I do not know – ever since he died.'

'He died? Your grandfather?'

'Did you not know? I was ill, very ill. My heart, the doctor said. It was I who should have died, but Grandfather would not hear of it. He said the doctor was a fool, he would save me himself. And he did. Yes, he did. He nursed and took care of me, even after I was in a coma.

'Then, when at last I was awake again, Grandfather failed. He was so old, you know. Caring for me without thought of himself – going without food or rest – it weakened him. Pneumonia set in and I could do nothing. He died here in the shop. That was a long time ago, it seems.'

'How long?'

'I cannot remember. I have not eaten or slept since, but then there is no need. I knew you would come—'

'Let me look at you.' I groped through the darkness, found the switch for the lamp over the workbench. The halo of light blossomed against the silent clock-faces on the walls.

Lisa stood there quietly, her face white and waxen, her eyes blank and empty, her body wasted. But she lived. That was enough for me. She lived, and she was free forever of the old man's tyranny.

I wondered what he had done to save her, he who had boasted that nothing would ever take her away from him. Well, he had lavished the last of his skill and genius upon preserving her from death, and it was enough.

I sighed and took Lisa in my arms. Her flesh was cold against mine, and I strove to melt the icy numbness against the heat of my body. I bent my head against her breast, listened to the beating of her heart.

· Then I turned and ran screaming from that shop of shadows and silence.

But not before I heard the hellish sound from Lisa's breast — that sound which was not a heartbeat, but a faint, unmistakable ticking.

EDIFICE COMPLEX

WAYNE looked at Nora and laughed.

'You're a good kid,' he said.

Nora's smile was bleary. Even though the ship was in grav, she had difficulty standing because she was bashed to the gills.

'You keep saying that, but you never do nothing. I thought this was a pleasure trip,' she giggled.

'Wait until we land,' Wayne reassured her. 'I told you last night when I brought you aboard, we can't do anything in free-fall. Besides, you've got your pay.'

Nora staggered over and put her plump hand on his shoulder as he bent over the scanner. Her voice was soft. 'I was hoping you wouldn't say that,' she murmured. 'I know what you think, picking me up in a stinking dive like that, but when I said yes, it wasn't just the money. I kind of went for you, hon, you know? And when you sweet-talked me into this I was thinking it would be, well, romantic like. Running off on your ship to a secret hideaway—'

She paused, blinking down into the scanner. They were cruising just a few thousand feet above the cloudless surface at a slow speed, circling over gentle, rolling sandy slopes with broad flat areas between. There was no water, no vegetation, no sign of life.

'Where are we, anyhow?' she asked.

'Vergis IV,' Wayne told her.

'Don't look like much of a place for a weekend,' Nora said. 'Lonely.'

Wayne grinned and pulled her close. 'That's just why I

picked it out,' he muttered. 'There'll be nobody around to bother you – except me.'

The plump, voluptuous brunette ran her hand along his spine. 'When you plan to start bothering, hon?' she whispered.

'Soon. Let me put us down first. I'm looking for a spot.'

Nora put her head close to his and stared into the scanner. 'Who told you about this place?' she asked.

'Friend of mine – a space-rat. Luke, they call him.'

The full-figured brunette giggled. 'Old Luke? The guy who hit Port City last week for a big bash-out? The one with all them diamonds?'

'That's right,' Wayne answered. 'Diamonds.'

'He sure was tossing 'em around. Dorine, she's my girlfriend, she was with him night before last. He was real bashed, and Dorine tried to find out where he got the loot. But he wasn't talking.'

'He told me,' Wayne said. 'The diamonds came from here.'

Nora dug her nails into his arm.

'Is that why you picked this place, on account of the diamonds?' Her breath quickened, and Wayne could smell the sickly-sweet odor of bash. 'You gonna get me some diamonds, hon?'

Wayne smiled down on her. 'I said you were a good kid, didn't I? If there are any diamonds here, you'll get them.'

'Oh, hon—'

'Hold it,' Wayne told her, disengaging her arms. 'We land first, remember? Meanwhile, how are you fixed for bash? I've got some prime stuff here in the pouch.'

'Sure, hon. Give me a pop. The more I bash, the better I am – you'll see—'

Wayne pulled the pouch from his pocket and poured a minute mound of the grayish seeds into her palm. She raised it to her nostrils and sniffed, inhaling with a deep sigh that ended in a sneeze.

'Now I'm cruising,' she said. The whites of her eyes turned yellow as the pupils contracted. 'Come on, hon—'

'Let me set us down,' Wayne urged. He squinted through the scanner. 'Right over there,' he told her.

'What's that big brown thing?' Nora asked, trying to focus her gaze. 'Looks like a snake.'

Wayne studied the brown, irregular oblong. 'It does at that, from this height,' he agreed. 'But it's really a hut. Luke told me to find a hut if I wanted to get hold of the natives. Besides, we'll need a place to stay.'

'How about right here on the ship?' Nora suggested. 'Right here on the ship, and right now—' She was beginning to breathe heavily.

'Don't forget the diamonds,' Wayne reminded.

'Diamonds.' Nora's voice trailed off as the bash took hold. She fell back upon the bunk. 'Hon, I'm dizzy. Don't leave me, hon.'

'I wouldn't think of it,' Wayne assured her. 'You're a good kid, remember?'

He grinned and bent over the controls. Slowly, the ship glided in for a landing on a sandy plain only a few hundred yards from the brown oblong. As Nora murmured incoherently, Wayne put out the landing platform and packed a small kit-bag which he slung over his shoulder. Then he stepped over to Nora and shook her.

'Wake up,' he said. 'We're going out.'

Eyes closed, Nora tried to pull him down on the bunk. 'Wait, hon,' she whispered. 'Let's not go now.'

'We've got to,' he told her. 'The way I figure it, there's less than an hour of daylight left. I want to look around.'

'You promised—'

'First let's see about the diamonds. If there's anybody in that hut they'll spot us.'

He raised the girl to her feet. She had to hang on to him as they walked down the ramp, and her legs went rubbery as she waded through the sand.

'Take your shoes off,' he suggested.

She kicked them aside. 'Hot,' Nora murmured, eyes closed against the sun's glare. 'Too hot.'

'Cooler in the hut,' he replied. 'Come on.'

They trudged over to the oblong. It was perhaps thirty feet in length, seven or eight feet high, and nine feet wide. Seen at close range it no longer resembled a serpent, except to Nora's bash-distorted vision.

'Looks creepy,' she whispered. 'What's it made of, anyway?'

'Some kind of hide, I guess. See how it's stretched? Wonder how they pieced it together—'

Wayne broke off as Nora stumbled against him. The girl was bashed, all right. Maybe he shouldn't have given her that last pop. But she was a good kid, he had to remember that.

And now, where were the natives?

He approached the dark doorway of the hut and tried to peer into the dimness beyond. There didn't seem to be any door at all, and no windows. The interior flooring slanted down away from the opening and he couldn't see very far within.

'Place must be deserted, all right,' he said. 'Let's take a peek inside.'

Nora tugged at his arm. 'I don't want to go in there. It's too dark.'

'Here's a light.' Wayne produced a small tube from his pack. 'Got a stunner attachment, too, following the beam. We're ready for anything.' He pulled her toward the doorway.

'It smells so,' the girl whimpered. 'Like snakes. And I think someone's looking at us.'

Wayne glanced behind him, scanning the desert horizon, then shook his head. 'You're just bash-happy.'

'I'm scared, that's all.'

He shrugged and moved forward. She had no choice but to follow. They walked down the slanting floor into the hut.

It did smell in here, Wayne realized. The odor was atrocious. No wonder the place was deserted. He swept the beam up and over the rough, unfinished walls. There was no furnishing, no sign of occupancy.

They stood in the outer chamber and gazed forward, noting that the interior of the hut was divided into several sections. Ahead of them was a narrow passageway leading to a second chamber. As Wayne moved forward the odor grew stronger and the girl held back.

'Let's go outside,' she urged. 'I'm choking, hon.' Wayne shook his head and advanced to the head of the passageway. He stood there and played his beam on the empty chamber beyond. The stench was almost intolerable, and it seemed to be coming from the floor, which was inches deep in stagnant muck. Maybe the natives used this hut as a cesspool. Maybe this is where they disposed of the—

'Look!' Nora had crept close behind him, and now she was cowering against him and pointing. 'See, in that slime in the corner? There's bones, and a skull!'

Wayne swept the beam around, away from the opening. 'You're imagining things,' he told her.

But he'd seen them too, and now he knew everything was all right.

'Want to go back outside?' he asked.

'Yes. Oh, please, hurry – I think I'm going to be sick.'

He half-supported Nora as she staggered back up the slanting slope leading to the doorway. The sky had darkened over the desert beyond, and the air was suddenly chill.

'Take a deep breath,' he commanded. 'You'll feel better.'

'Not until we get back to the ship,' the girl whispered. 'I can't stand being near this place. There's something awful about it. It isn't just a house, it's—' Abruptly she paused and stared back at the oblong bulk of the hut. 'We're being watched,' she said. 'I know it.'

'Nonsense. You can see for yourself there's nobody around.'

'Then where are the natives?'

'Hunting, perhaps.'

'Are there animals around, too?'

149

'No.'

'Then what do they hunt?'

'Each other.'

'You mean they're—'

'Cannibals.' Wayne nodded. 'It's a dying world. No real civilization. No wonder they give diamonds as gifts. They're so grateful when anyone brings them a present.'

'Is that how Luke got his loot?' Nora asked. 'What kind of present did he give them?'

Wayne grinned at her. 'His partner, Brady.'

Nora's mouth twitched. 'You're joking. Or – he was lying to you—'

'Dying men don't lie,' Wayne said, softly. 'I picked old Luke up in an alley, two nights ago, bashed to the lungs and coughing his guts out. Dragged him into my place, and ten minutes later he was dead. But he talked, first. I thought he was delirious, until I saw the diamonds. Then I knew he was telling the truth.

'It had all been an accident, really. He and Brady were scavengers, operating a little wildcat freighter. They were on their way back from Cybele when Luke got sick. Brady must have figured it was better to find a place to stop, and he put down here. Luke was unconscious at the time.

'When he came to, he was alone on the freighter. Apparently Brady had decided to step out and take a look around. It was night, but the moon was up and Luke could see out – he was in desert country, like this. And there was nobody around. Off in the distance was one of these huts, and Luke wondered if Brady had gone to investigate. He felt pretty weak, but he just about made up his mind to follow his partner when the natives came.

'Luke didn't let them get aboard, of course. But he stood in the airlock and gestured at them. I guess they caught on to his sign language in a hurry. Anyway, they nodded at him and pantomimed. The way it looked, they'd found Brady wandering outside and jumped him.

'Luke said there were a dozen or more of them, all carrying long spears. He couldn't possibly handle them all, so he did the next best thing – smiled, looked friendly, and tried to find out what they'd done with Brady.

'So he made stabbing gestures and cutting gestures, but they just shook their heads and kept gesturing over at the hut in the distance. Then some of them bowed down facing it, and the rest bowed down facing the ship. And the biggest one, whom Luke took to be the chief, pulled out the sack of diamonds. He set it down and bowed again. Then he pointed at the hut once more and started to rub his belly. That's when Luke guessed the rest. You see, he thought Luke was some kind of god who had brought them Brady as an offering. And they were repaying him in diamonds.'

The moon was rising redly over the black bulk of the hut, and Wayne could see Nora's face flaming in the light. Her eyes were glazed.

'The natives left, then, and after a while Luke opened the lock and picked up the diamonds. He wanted to go to the hut and find Brady, but he was afraid. Instead, he took off. That's why he went on the bash when he hit port. He knew he'd been a coward.'

'I don't believe it,' Nora murmured. 'He was out of his head.'

'I saw the diamonds,' Wayne reminded her.

'But it doesn't make sense. Maybe he and Brady found diamonds here and they quarreled. So he killed his partner and took the loot for himself. That crazy yarn about the natives eating each other—'

'You saw the bones in the hut,' Wayne muttered. 'And in a little while, you'll see the natives, too.'

Nora stepped back. 'I don't want to see them,' she wailed. 'I want to go back to the ship. Why did you bring me here in the first place? Why—'

'Because you're a good kid,' Wayne said, and hit her across the face with his flash.

She fell forward heavily and he put his knee in her back, pressing her down as he got the rope out of his pack. The bash had weakened her and she couldn't put up much of a struggle.

He tied her wrists expertly and then dragged her along the sand by her ankles. She moaned a little, but didn't come around until he'd propped her up on a small rise a few hundred feet from the entrance to the hut.

'There we are,' he told her. 'All wrapped and ready. Like I said, you're a good kid. But I suppose you don't know what I mean, do you?'

'Hon, let me go—'

'A kid is a baby goat. Once upon a time, back on Terra, in a place called India, there were other animals called tigers. Some of them were man-eaters. When the natives wanted to attract a man-eater, they staked a kid out.

'So when I heard Luke's story, I knew what to do. I started looking for bait for a man-eater, and I found you.'

'You can't—'

'I can.' Wayne stared down at her soberly. 'Nobody saw us together last night. Nobody knows you sneaked off with me on an unauthorized flight. The Port is filled with tramps like you – they come and go. Even if somebody notices your disappearance, I'll never be involved.'

'But why me?' she was sobbing now, wheezing in panic.

Wayne reached forward and started ripping away her garments, slowly and deliberately.

'This is why,' he murmured. 'Because you're white and soft. Because you're plump and rounded and tender. Because you're a good kid.'

'Stop! Let me go!'

Wayne stood up, nodding. 'That's right,' he said. 'Go ahead and scream. If they don't see that body of yours in the moonlight, at least they'll hear your voice. When the kid bleats, the man-eater comes.'

'No – don't leave me – come back – I'll do anything you want, anything!'

'You'll get me the diamonds,' Wayne told her. 'I'll be waiting, never fear.'

He walked over to the dark shadow of the oblong hut and

crouched just inside the doorway. The charnel stench was strong on the night air, but he wanted to keep out of sight. After they came, that was the psychological moment. With the weapon in his hand, he had nothing to fear. They'd treated old Luke like a god, and he'd get the same consideration.

Nora was crying softly in the distance. Her nude body was radiant in the moonlight. If there were any natives around, they'd be here soon.

For a moment he wondered if Nora had been right. Could the old scavenger have made up the whole yarn just as she said? Maybe there were no natives after all. The whole idea of cannibals with spears seemed a bit naïve and ridiculous. Brady could have wandered off, found some diamonds, then brought them back with him. Maybe he'd tried to hide them from his partner, only to have Luke discover them and kill him in a quarrel over the loot. That made a lot more sense.

Yes, the old space-rat had probably been lying. And who could blame him under the circumstances? Wayne hadn't told Nora the whole story – what he'd gotten out of Luke at the end wasn't a voluntary confession. Sure, he'd picked the old man up in the alley and dragged him inside, but only after he'd gone through the dying man's pockets and found the diamonds. That's why he put him on his bed, and started choking him; choking him until the story came out in bits and pieces, like the bits and pieces of lung he coughed up in the final dying spasm.

Wayne frowned at himself. He'd been a little too rough; otherwise he'd have gotten more of the details. He'd have found out how to separate fact from fancy. As it was, all he really knew was that Luke had found the diamonds here on Vergis IV.

If there was nothing to the yarn about the cannibal natives, then Wayne was wasting his time. He'd have to dispose of the girl himself and then go diamond-hunting.

On the other hand, he reminded himself, there were the huts, just like Luke described them. Someone must have built them. And now he remembered the bones. The bones and the stench. There had to be man-eaters around. There had to be—

A whiff of carrion odor caused him to wrinkle his nose in revulsion. He wished there was another place of concealment available. Nora had been right; something about this hut made him feel uneasy. What kind of creatures could have built it? Where did they get the hides? Maybe they used their own skins – that is, the skins of their victims. Wayne tried to imagine a completely cannibalistic civilization. Had there ever been any on Terra?

Wayne tried to think about that for a moment, but there was something else that disturbed him, something he couldn't quite account for.

Maybe it was the red moon. It gave him the feeling Nora had complained about in the hut, the feeling of being watched. It was too much like an accusing eye.

Maybe it was remembering how he'd choked the story out of that bash-crazed old man; maybe it was seeing that naked, moaning girl up there on the rise.

He stared at her silhouette as it writhed on the horizon and wondered when something was going to happen. He hoped it would be soon, because he had to get out of here, the smell was getting worse—

Suddenly Wayne stiffened and crouched back in the doorway.

Something was coming over the rim of the hill.

The bait was luring the man-eater.

Wayne squinted into the wastes, trying to distinguish individual forms in the black blur that moved across the hilltop. Why, there must be an army of them, moving packed together in a solid mass!

Nora saw the movement too, because she was screaming, now. And there was another sound – a soft, slow rumbling. The black bulk was flowing forward. It wasn't black, really; more of a reddish brown. The same color as the hut.

Then Wayne realized why he couldn't make out individual figures. There were no figures – just the solid mass. The thing crawling sluggishly over the hillside was a single great form. A brown oblong form, moving slowly but surely.

As Wayne recognized the object, another realization came to him. Now he knew what had eluded his mind. It was something about this hut. With no wind to disturb the sand, why hadn't he noticed the footprints of the natives leading to and from the doorway?

He had the answer, now. There were no natives – at least, no humanoid cannibals. Nora's guess had been correct. Brady found the diamonds and Luke killed him, then made up the story about natives dragging him into their hut. Brady hadn't been dragged to a hut – *the hut had come to him.*

And it was coming to Nora, now, out there on the hillside, its brown bulk inching toward her, towering over her, the black doorway gaping to engulf her like a ravenous mouth.

But it is a mouth, Wayne told himself, and suddenly there was a shock of final recognition as he remembered the hide-like covering that was hide, and the second inner compartment with the stagnant stench bubbling over the bones.

The huts were man-eaters, and he had to get out of here! He moved up the slanting slope leading to the doorway, eyes intent on the spectacle before him. Nora was screaming, the maw was closing over her – and then the vision was blotted out.

The maw was closing over him.

The doorway ahead of him disappeared, and the slanting slope moved beneath his feet. It contracted in a series of ripples, convulsing like a throat in the act of swallowing. Wayne gasped, the stench suddenly stronger in his nostrils. He clawed out at the walls, dropping his weapon as the slope tilted, pushing him back. And now a wave of nauseous liquid gushed out from the floor, and Wayne felt himself forced back, thinking idiotically, *salivation, that's what is is,* and wondering why there were no teeth in the house.

The odor was overpowering, and he felt the slimy waves wash over him as he retreated, forcing his way along the narrow passage toward the second chamber.

It squeezed him clammily, and all too late he realized that this must be the esophagus.

Snakes. Nora had said. The thing smelled like a snake, it looked like a snake, it was a snake. A snake that devours its victims whole and alive. And then digests them in its stomach.

Wayne clawed the constricting walls of the narrow passage, trying to hold himself back. But the creature was moving and shuddering all around him, and then it gave a great gulp and swallowed. Wayne fell into the second compartment, and the bubbling liquid surged and seared . . .

When daylight came, the hut was sluggish and quiescent. The dark doorway opened once more, but there was no other sign of movement.

The hut belched once, then settled back to wait.

CONSTANT READER

ONCE upon a time they were called strait jackets.

When you put one on, you were 'in restraint' according to the polite psychiatric jargon of the day. I know, because I've read all about it in books. Yes, real books, the old-fashioned kind that were printed on paper and bound together between leather or board covers. They're still available in some libraries, Earthside, and I've read a lot of them. As a matter of fact, I own quite a collection myself. It's a peculiar hobby, but I enjoy it much more than telolearning or going to the sensorals.

Of course, I admit I'm a little bit maladjusted, according to those same psychiatric texts I mentioned. That's the only possible explanation of why I enjoy reading, and why I pick up so many odd items of useless information.

This business about strait jackets and restraint, for example. All I ever got out of it was a peculiar feeling whenever we hit grav, on a Rec. Flight.

I got it again, now, as Penner yelled, 'Act alert, Dale – put down that toy and strap up!'

I dropped my book and went over to the Sighter Post. Already I could feel the preliminary pull despite the neutralizer's efforts. I strapped up and hung there in my cocoon, hung there in my strait jacket.

There I was, nicely in restraint, in our own little private asylum – Scout #3890-R, two months out of Home Port 19/1, and now approaching 68/5 planet for Reconnaissance.

Before looking out of the Sighter, I took another glance at my fellow inmates. Penner, Acting Chief, Temp., was strapped in at Mechontrol; all I could see of him was the broad back, the bullet head bent in monomaniac concentration. Swanson, Astrog., 2nd Class, hung at his side, cake-knife nose in profile over the Obsetape. Little Morse, Tech., was stationed at my left and old Levy, Eng., hung to my right. All present and accounted for – Penner, Swanson, Morse, Levy and myself. George Dale, Constant Reader and erstwhile Service Observer, hanging in his strait jacket after two months in a floating madhouse.

Two months of anything is a long time. Two months of Rec. Flight is an eternity. Being cooped up with four other men in a single compartment for that length of time is no picnic, and our strait jackets seemed singularly appropriate.

Not that any of us were actually psycho; all of us had a long record of similar missions, and we managed to survive. But the sheer monotony had worn us down.

I suppose that's why Service gave us the extra seven pounds per man – Lux. Allotment, it was called. But the so-called luxuries turn out to be necessities after all. Swanson usually put his poundage into solid food; candy, and the like. Chocolate capsules kept him sane. Morse and Levy went in for games – cards, dice, superchess and the necessary boards. Penner, amazingly enough, did sketching on pads of old-fashioned paper. And I had this habit of my own – I always managed to bring three or four books within the weight limit.

I still think my choice was the best; candy-munching, freehand sketching and the delights of dicing and superchessmanship palled quickly enough on my four companions. But the books kept me interested. I had a peculiar background – learned to read as a child rather than as an adult – and I guess that's why I derived such queer satisfaction from my hobby.

Naturally, the others laughed at me. Naturally, we got on each other's nerves, quarreled and fretted and flared up. But now, resting quietly in our strait jackets as we entered grav, a measure of sanity returned. With it came anticipation and expectation.

We were approaching 68/5 planet.

New worlds to conquer? Not exactly. It was a new world, and therein lay the expectation. But we weren't out to conquer, we on Rec. Flight merely observed and recorded. Or, rather, our instruments recorded.

At the moment we slid in on Mechontrol, about five hundred miles above the surface. 68/5 was small, cloud-wreathed; it had atmosphere apparently, as did its companions. Now we were moving closer and we peered through the Sighters at a dull, flat surface that seemed to be rushing towards us at accelerating speed.

'Pretty old,' little Morse grunted. 'No mountains, and no water, either – dried up, I guess.'

'No life.' This from old Levy. 'That's a relief.' Levy was what the books would have called a misanthrope. Although his mis wasn't confined to anthropes. He seemed to have a congenital aversion to everything that wasn't strictly mechanical – why he didn't stick to robotics, I'll never know.

We came down faster. Fifty miles, forty, thirty. I saw Swanson making arrangements to drop the roboship. Penner gave the signal as he righted us above the surface. The roboship glided away, guided by Swanson at the Obsetape. It drifted down, down, down. We followed slowly, dropping below the cloud barrier and following it closely.

'Hit!' snapped Swanson. 'Right on the button.' We waited while the roboship did its job. It was our star reporter, our roving photographer, our official meteorologist, our staff geologist, our expert in anthropology and mineralogic, our trusted guide and – most important, on many occasions – our stalking-horse.

If there was life present on a planet, the landing of the roboship generally brought it forth. If there was death on a planet, the roboship found it for us. And always, it recorded. It was, in a way, a complete expedition encapsulated, a non-human functional without the human capability of error or terror.

Now it went into action, cruising over the surface, directed by Swanson's delicate manipulation of the Obsetape unit controls. We waited patiently, then impatiently. An hour passed, two hours.

'Bring it in!' Penner ordered. Swanson moved his fingers and the roboship returned.

Penner snapped on the Temporary Balance. 'Everybody unstrap,' he said. 'Let's take a look!'

We went down the ramp to the lower deck and Swanson opened the roboship. The photos were ready, the tapes were spooled. We were busy with findings for another hour. At the end of that time we had all the preliminary data necessary on 68/5 planet.

Oxygen content high. Gravity similar to Earthside – as seemed constant in this particular sector and system. No detectable life forms. But life had existed here, once, and life of a high order. The photos proved that. City ruins galore.

And the planet was old. No doubt about that. Morse had been right; mountains were worn away to dust, and the dust did not support vegetable life. Strange that the oxygen content was still so high. I'd have supposed that carbonization—

'Let's snap out,' Penner said. 'We don't need Temporary Balance or straps according to the gravity reading. Might as well go in for a landing right away. The day-cycle here is 20.1 hours – computer gives us a good 5 hours to go, right now. So we can all take a look around.'

We filed back upstairs and Swanson brought us in.

It was only a dead planet, a desert of dust without trees or grass or water; a flat, slate-colored surface where everything was the same, same, same. But it was solid, you could put your feet down on it, you could walk across the sand for miles and feel the air flow against your face.

And there were ruins to explore. That might be interesting. At least, it was a change.

I could feel the tension and excitement mount; it was as palpable as the momentary shock and shudder of landing. We crowded around the lock, struggling out of our suits and putting on the light plastikoids, buckling on the gear and weapons as prescribed by regulation. Morse handed us our equipment and we zipped and strapped and adjusted in a frenzy of impatience. Even Penner was eager, but he remembered to grab his sketchpad before the lock was opened.

Normally, I suppose he would have insisted on maintaining a watch on board, but in the absence of life it didn't really matter. And after two months, everybody wanted out.

The lock opened. The ladder went down. We inhaled, deeply, turned our faces to the warmth of the distant orange sun.

'Single file – keep together!' Penner cautioned.

It's the last day of school, and dismissal is sounded, and the boys rush out onto the playground. So the teacher warns, 'Single file – keep together!' and what happens?

Just what happened now. In a moment we were racing across the soft sand, grinning and tossing handfuls of the fine grains high into the clean, dry air. We ran across the brand-new world on our brand-new legs.

We moved in the direction we couldn't help thinking of as west – because the orange sun hung there and we turned to the sun as naturally as flowers recently transplanted from a hothouse.

We moved buoyantly and joyfully and freely, for this was vacation and picnic and release from the asylum all in one. The smiles on the faces of my companions bespoke euphoria. It was all good: the gritty, sliding sand under our feet, the pumping of legs in long strides, the grinding ball-and-socket action of the hips, the swinging of the arms, the rise and fall of the chest, the lungs greedily gasping in and squandering recklessly, the eyes seeing far, far away. Yes, it was good to be here, good to be alive, good to be free.

Once again we measured minutes in terms of movements, rather than abstract units of time-passage we must endure. Once again we consciously heightened our awareness of existence, rather than dulled it to make life bearable.

It seemed to me that I'd never felt so completely alive, but I was wrong. I was wrong, because I didn't notice the blackout.

None of us were aware of it: even now, I can't begin to comprehend it. I don't know what happened. It was just that – blackout.

Before it happened, we marched towards the sun – Penner, Swanson and Morse a little in the lead, Levy and I a pace or two behind, all of us trudging up a slight incline in the sand.

And then, without any seeming transition at all, we were marching in darkness – Penner, Swanson, Morse, Levy and I in a solid group, trudging down into a valley.

'What happened?'

'Eclipse?'

'Where's the sun?'

'Where are we?'

'How long we been walking? I feel like I passed out.'

We halted and exchanged comments.

'Something wrong here. We're going back. Get out the beamers.' Penner issued orders swiftly.

We broke out the beamers, adjusted the slow-strobes, put pathways of light before us. There was nothing to see but slaty sand. Only Swanson's bearings with the scope guided us in retracing our steps. We moved swiftly through the pall of a purple night. A mist shrouded the stars; a mist mantled our memories.

That's when we compared notes, realized for the first time that the phenomenon had occurred to all of us simultaneously. Gas, shock, temporary dislocation – we argued about the cause for hours, and all the while we marched on the alert, up hummocks and down into little valleys between the dunes.

And we were tired. Unused muscles strained, hearts pumped, feet blistered, and still we marched. I was hungry and thirsty and tired; more than that, I was puzzled and a little bit afraid. I didn't understand just what had happened – how could we, all of us, go on walking that way while we were out on our feet? How could we lose almost four hours? And what did it mean?

At the moment we were in no danger of being lost, and it was more and more obvious that this planet contained no life, hostile or otherwise. But why the blackout? It puzzled me, puzzled all of us.

Swanson took the lead. His beak-like profile loomed on a rise in my beamer's path. He turned and yelled, 'I can see the ship now!'

We toiled up the slope and joined him. Yes, the ship was there, snug and safe and secure, and the adventure was over.

Or – was it?

'Look down there!' Levy swivelled his beamer to the left. 'We must have missed it on the way out.'

Five rays played, pooled, pointed in a single beam. Five rays found, focused and flooded upon the objects rising from the sand. And then we were all running together towards the ruins.

Just before we reached them, Penner yelled, 'Stop!'

'What's wrong?' I said.

'Nothing – maybe. Then again, you never know. That blackout bothers me.' Penner put his hand on my shoulder. 'Look, Dale, I want you and Morse to go back to the ship and wait. The three of us will take a trip through the ruins. But I want at least two men on ship at all times, in case there's any trouble. Go ahead, now – we won't move until we see you're on board. Flash us a signal to let us know everything's all right when you get there.'

Morse and I trudged off.

'Just my luck,' little Morse grumbled under his breath and waved his beamer in disgust. 'Run around for hours in the sand and then when we finally hit something it's back to the ship. Huh!'

'He's right, though,' I answered. 'Got to be careful. And besides, we can eat and take our shoes off.'

'But I want to see those ruins. Besides, I promised my girl some souvenirs—'

'Tomorrow we'll probably get our turn,' I reminded him. He shrugged and plodded on. We reached the ship, boarded, and took a quick look around. All clear.

Morse went over to the panel and pushed the blinker. Then we sat down next to the Sighter and stared out. All we could see at this distance was a purple blur, through which three beams moved and wavered.

I opened foodcaps and we swallowed, still straining to see. The lights moved separately at first, then coalesced into a single unit.

'Must have found something,' Morse speculated. 'Wonder what?'

'We'll find out soon enough,' I predicted.

But they didn't come back, and they didn't come back – we sat for hours, waiting.

Finally the beams moved our way. We were waiting as Penner, Swanson and Levy boarded. An excited babble wavered into words and the words became sentences.

'Never saw anything like them—'

'Smaller than dwarfs; couldn't be, but I'd swear they were human.'

'Gets me is the way they disappeared, just like somebody had scooped them all up at once.'

'Wasn't their city, I'm sure of that. First of all, it was ages old, and secondly it wasn't built to their size-scale at all—'

'Think we just imagined the whole thing? That blackout was peculiar enough, and then, seeing them this way—'

I raised my voice. 'What's all this about? What did you find?'

The answer was more babbling in unison, until Penner signalled for silence.

'See what you make of this, Dale,' he said. He pulled out his sketch-pad and went to work, swiftly. As he worked, he talked. Story and sketches emerged almost simultaneously.

He passed the first drawing to me.

'Ruins,' he said. 'Ruins of a city. All we really saw were the rooftops, but they're enough to give you some idea of the probable size of the place. You'll note everything was solid stone. Plenty of broad, flat surfaces. Here's a sketch of me standing between two rooftops. Probably a street in between, at one time. What do you make of it?'

I studied his sketch; it was crude, but graphically explicit. 'They must have been humanoid,' I said. 'If we accept functionalism in architectural representation—'

'Never mind the book words,' Penner interrupted. 'Look at the width of that street. Would you say that the inhabitants were large or small?'

'Large, of course.' I looked at the sketch again. 'Must have been much taller than we are, perhaps seven or eight feet if they worked according to our proportions. Of course, that's just a rough guess.'

'Good enough. And we geigered the stones a bit. Levy, here, places them at fourteen thousand years.'

'The very least,' Levy broke in. 'Possibly older than that.'

Penner was sketching again. He passed the second drawing over to me. 'Here's what we found wandering around in the ruins,' he told me. 'I've shown two of them standing next to me, but there must have been hundreds.'

I looked. There stood Penner, and – at his feet – two tiny man-like beings.

'You actually saw these things?'

'Of course. We all did, there's no doubt about it. One minute we were climbing around among the stones, and then they appeared. Just like that, out of nowhere, you might say. And not one or two, but hundreds of them.' He turned. 'Isn't that right, Swanson?'

'Correct.'

I gazed at the sketch again. Penner had an eye for detail. I was particularly impressed with the way the creatures were dressed.

'These look like ancient earth-garments,' I said. 'They're

wearing little armoured breastplates, and helmets. And they carry spears.'

'That's exactly how they looked,' Levy corroborated. 'Some of them had those – what were they called? – bows and arrows.'

Penner eyed me. 'You've got a theory, Dale?'

'No, but I'm getting one. These little things never built the city. They don't live in the ruins, now. They couldn't possibly wear earth-garments like these. They appeared suddenly, you say, and disappeared just as suddenly.'

'Sounds silly, the way you sum it up,' Penner admitted.

'Yes. Unless you accept one over-all theory.'

'And that is?'

'That they don't exist! They never existed at all, except in your imagination.'

'But we all saw them. Saw them, and heard them!'

'We all went through a blackout together, a few hours ago,' I reminded him. 'And I'm beginning to think that ties in, somehow. Suppose 68/5 isn't uninhabited. Suppose it does contain life.'

'That's out of the question!' Swanson interrupted. 'The roboship tapes are infallible. Any signs of existence would have been detected and recorded. You know that.'

'Yet suppose there were no signs,' I answered. 'Suppose we're dealing with an intangible intelligence—'

'Absurd!' This from Penner.

'No more absurd than the story you've told me. Suppose the intelligence can control our minds. It blacked us out and planted hypnotic suggestion. A little while later you saw little men—'

'No. It doesn't add up,' Levy insisted. 'There's a flaw.' He pointed at the second sketch. 'How would your intelligence know about earth garments such as these? I'm sure none of us were aware of such things. You're the bookworm around here—'

'Bookworm!' I paused. 'Wait a minute. You say these creatures talked to you?'

'That's right,' Penner answered.

'Do you remember any of the words?'

'I think so. They had little shrill voices and they were shouting to each other. Sounded something like *Hekinah degul* and *Langro dehul san*.'

'One of them pointed at you and said *Hurgo* over and over,' Swanson reminded him.

'*Hurgo*,' I repeated. 'Wait a minute.' I walked over to my shelf and pulled down one of my books. 'Look at this,' I said. 'No pictures in this edition, of course, but read this page.'

Penner read slowly as the others crowded around. He raised his head, scowled. 'Sounds like our creatures,' he said. 'What is this?'

I turned to the frontispiece and read: '*Gulliver's Travels*, by Jonathan Swift. Published, 1727.'

'No!' said Penner.

I shrugged. 'It's all in the book,' I told him. 'Descriptions, words, phrases. Some intelligent force out there tried to read our minds and – I think – failed. So it read the book, instead, and reproduced a part of it.'

'But what possible force could exist? And how could it read the book? And why did it reproduce the—' Penner halted, groping for the word which I supplied.

'Lilliputians.'

'All right, why did it reproduce Lilliputians?'

I didn't know the answers. I couldn't even guess. All I had was a feeling, which I expressed in one short sentence. 'Let's get out of here.'

Penner shook his head. 'We can't. You know that. We've stumbled across something without precedent, and it's our job to investigate it fully. Who knows what we might learn? I say we get some rest and go back tomorrow.'

There was a mumble of agreement. I had nothing more to say, so I kept quiet. Swanson and Morse and Levy sought their bunks. I started across to mine, when Penner tapped me on the shoulder.

'By the way, Dale, would you mind letting me have that book

of yours? I want to read up on those creatures – might come in handy tomorrow.'

I gave him the book and he went forward. Then I lay down and prepared to sleep. Before closing my eyes I took a last look out of the nearest Sighter. The planet was dark and dead. There was nothing out there – nothing but sand and ruins and loneliness. And something that made up Lilliputians, something that read in order to learn, and learned in order to plan, and planned in order to act—

I didn't get much sleep that night.

The sun was lemon-colored the next morning when Swanson roused us.

'Come on,' he said. 'Penner says we're going out again. Two of us will stay on ship, but we'll take turns. Morse, you and Dale can get ready.'

'Orders?' I asked.

'No. I don't think so. It's just that it's really your turn to see the ruins.'

I faced him. 'I don't want to see the ruins. And my advice is that we all stay on ship and blast off, right now.'

'What's the trouble?' Penner loomed up behind Swanson.

'He doesn't want to go out,' Swanson said. 'Thinks we ought to leave.' He smiled at Penner, and said, 'Coward.'

Penner grinned at me and his grin said, 'Psycho.'

I didn't let my face talk for me. This was serious. 'Look, now,' I began. 'I've been awake most of the night, thinking. And I've got a hunch.'

'Let's hear it.' Penner was courteous enough, but over his shoulder he said, 'Meanwhile, why don't you men get into your suits?'

'This intelligence we talked about last night – we all agreed it must exist. But it can't be measured or located.'

'That's what we're going to try to do this morning,' Penner said.

'I advise against it.'

'Go on.'

'Let's think about intelligence for a moment. Ever try to define it? Pretty difficult thing to do. We all know there are hundreds of worlds that don't contain intelligence but do contain life. New worlds and old worlds alike have a complete existence and cycle independent of conscious intelligence.'

'What's this, a book lecture?' asked Morse.

'No, just my own ideas. And one of my ideas is that what we call intelligence is a random element, arising spontaneously under certain conditions just as life itself does. It isn't necessary for the existence of a world – it's extraneous, it's a parasite, an alien growth. Usually it uses brain cells as a host. But suppose it could evolve to the point where it isn't limited to brain cells?'

'All right, then what?' Penner snapped.

'Suppose, when life dies on a planet, intelligence finds a means of survival? Suppose it adapts itself to something other than the tissue of the cortex? Suppose the highest point of evolution is reached – in which the planet itself, as host, becomes the seat of intelligence?'

'Mean to say that 68/5 can think?'

'It's worth considering. Remember, when intelligence enters brain cells it identifies itself with its host, and tries in every way to help its host survive. Suppose it enters, finally, into the planet – when life dies out – and tries to help the planet survive?'

'Thinking planets! Now I've heard everything!' This from Swanson. 'Dale, you read too many books.'

'Perhaps. But consider what's happened. We can't locate any life-form here. Nevertheless, we black out. And something creates, out of reading and imagination, a duplicate of *Gulliver's Travels*. Think in terms of a combined number of intelligences, fused into a single unit housed in the body of this world itself. Think of its potential power, and then think of its motives. We're outsiders, we may be hostile, we must be controlled or destroyed. And that's what the planet is trying to do. It can't read our minds, but it can read my books. And its combined force is enough to materialize imaginative concepts in an effort to destroy us. First came little Lilliputians with bows and arrows and tiny spears. The intelligence realized these wouldn't be effective, so it may try something else. Something like—'

Penner cut me off with a gesture. 'All right, Dale. You don't have to come with us if you don't want to.' It was like a slap in the face. I stared around the circle. The men had their suits on. Nobody looked at me.

Then, surprisingly enough, Levy spoke up. 'Maybe he's right,' he said. 'Somebody else has to stay behind, too. Think I'll keep Dale company here.'

I smiled at him. He came over, unfastening his suit. The others didn't say anything. They filed over to the stairs.

'We'll watch you through the Sighters,' Levy said. Penner nodded, disappeared with the others.

Minutes later we caught sight of them toiling up the sun-baked slope of the ridge leading towards the ruins. In the clear light now the ruins were partially visible. Even though only rooftops were clear of sand, they looked gigantic and imposing. An ancient race had dwelt here. And now a new race had come. That was the way life went. Or death—

'What are you worrying about?' Levy asked. 'Stop squirming.'

'I don't like it,' I said. 'Something's going to happen. You believed me too or you wouldn't have stayed.'

'Penner's a fool,' Levy said. 'You know, I used to read a few books myself, once upon a time.'

'Once upon a time!' I stood up. 'I forgot!'

'Where are you going?'

'I'm looking for my other two books,' I said. 'I should have thought of that.'

'Thought of what?' Levy talked to me, but he was watching the others, outside, through the Sighter.

'If it read one book, it can read the others,' I told him. 'Better get rid of them right away, play it safe.'

'What are the other two books?' Levy asked the question, but

I never answered him. Because his voice changed, cracked, and he said, 'Dale, come here, hurry!'

I stared through the Sighter. I adjusted the control and it was like a closeup. I could see Penner and Swanson and Morse as if they were standing beside me. They had just reached the top of the ridge, and the ruined stones of the cyclopean city rose before them. *Cyclopean.*

The word came, the concept came, and then the reality. The first giant towered up from behind the rocks. He was thirty feet tall and his single eye was a burning beacon.

They saw him and turned to flee. Penner tugged at his waist, trying to draw his tube and fire. But there wasn't time now, for the giants were all around them – the bearded, one-eyed monsters out of myth.

The giants laughed, and their laughter shook the earth, and they scooped up great rocks from the ruins and hurled them at the men, crushing them. And then they lumbered over to the crushed forms and began to feast, their talons rending and tearing the bodies as I now tore the pages from the book I was holding.

'Cyclops,' Levy whispered. '*The Odyssey*, isn't it?' The torn fragments of the second book fell from my fingers as I turned away.

Levy was already working at the panels. 'Only two of us,' he said. 'But we can make it. Take-off's automatic once we blast. I'm pretty sure we can make it, aren't you, Dale?'

'Yes,' I said, but I didn't really care.

The floor was beginning to vibrate. In just a minute, now, we'd blast.

'Come on, Dale, strap up! I'll handle the board. You know what to do.'

I knew what to do.

Levy's face twitched. 'What's the matter now? Is it the third book? Are you going to get rid of the third book?'

'No need to. The third one's harmless,' I said. 'Here, I'll show you.'

'What is the third book?' he asked.

I stepped over to the Sighter for the last time and he followed me. I adjusted for closeup very carefully.

'Look,' I said.

We stared out across the barren plain, the plain which no longer held life because it had *become* life for this planet.

The Cyclops had disappeared, and what was left of Penner, and Swanson and Morse lay undisturbed in the dreaming ruins under an orange sun.

Somewhere, somehow, the reader turned a page—

'The third book,' I whispered. 'Watch.'

It scampered out from behind one of the stones, moving swiftly on tiny legs. The Sighter brought it so close that I could see the very hairs of its whiskers, note the design of its checkered waistcoat, read the numerals on the watch it took out of the waistcoat pocket. Before I turned away, I almost fancied I could read its lips.

That wasn't necessary of course, because I knew what it was saying.

'Oh dear! Oh dear! I shall be too late!' it murmured.

Mincing daintily on thin legs, the White Rabbit scampered among the bodies as we blasted off.

THE END

of an Original Gold Medal Collection by

Robert Bloch

PSYCHO BY ROBERT BLOCH

THE STORY THAT ALFRED HITCHCOCK MADE INTO HIS MOST SPINE-CHILLING FILM

She stepped into the shower stall. She let the warm water gush over her. That's why she didn't hear the door open. At first, when the shower curtains parted, steam obscured the face. Then she saw it . . .

A face peering through the curtains. A headscarf concealed the hair, and glassy eyes stared inhumanly. The skin was powdered dead-white and two spots of rouge were centered on the cheekbones.

She started to scream. Then the curtains parted further and a hand appeared, holding a butcher's knife . . .

0 552 10402 7   60p

FIREBUG BY ROBERT BLOCH

A FRIGHTENING LOOK INTO THE BLACK AND CHARRED SOUL OF A MANIAC

I was all alone, but somewhere out there in the city was another. A man I'd never met, but who knew about me, because he'd read about me in the papers. He'd know I was dangerous to his plans, and he was clever enough to act.

Schwarm, the head-shrinker, had said most firebugs were adolescent and subnormal. But these two crimes weren't the work of an adolescent, a kid doesn't kill five people intentionally. Abnormal would be the proper term. Abnormal and abnormally cunning. Cunning enough to throw a great city into panic every time somebody lights up a cigarette.

No, this wasn't arson, this was murder. And how many more ?

0 552 10403 5   60p

REIGN OF TERROR I EDITED BY MICHEL PARRY

'That the sixty-four year reign of Queen Victoria generated more than its share of horrors, no one can deny. The backstreets of Victorian London, those grim, overcrowded warrens of despair, were a bustling breeding ground of horror ... If this collection helps in some way to vindicate Victorian supernatural and horror fiction and return it to its rightful position of pre-eminence, I shall be well pleased. But to be honest, my principal aim in compiling these stories is somewhat more modest. Like Dickens' Fat Boy, "I only wants to make your flesh creep ..." '

From the introduction by Michel Parry in this first volume of scalp-tingling tales and macabre classics.

0 552 10335 7   65p

THE SKULL OF THE MARQUIS DE SADE BY ROBERT BLOCH

Once it held the most evil brain on Earth ... now it was a curiosity for collectors – a sinister-looking but harmless piece of polished bone, resting on a desk ...

But somehow, something happened to whoever owned it – or bought it – or stole it ...

And each in turn discovered – in the last seconds of his life – the secret of the SKULL OF THE MARQUIS DE SADE.

0 552 10234 2   50p

THE NATURE OF THE BEAST BY PETER MENEGAS

New York, London, Cornwall. Three settings. Three different worlds. Or are they just variations on hell? Dee-Dee Burke cannot find peace in any of these places.

Forces of evil are omnipresent and they are trying to steal her children. They are initiating her little boys into the primitive language and rituals of Celtic witchcraft. They have given her sons the gift of prophecy in exchange for perverse and inhuman acts of barbarism. Their power is more ancient than Christianity, more savage than Satanism. And they will succeed – unless Dee-Dee can bargain to save her children's lives . . .

0 552 10147 1   75p

DAUGHTER OF DARKNESS BY J. R. LOWELL

Willie was different from other little girls, she was pretty, highly intelligent and very, very evil . . . Willie didn't want to go on a class outing to the Museum of Natural History . . . and, miraculously, her science teacher fell ill so the trip had to be postponed . . . Willie wanted a pet cat. . . . but her mother gave her a puppy instead. Soon the puppy was run over and killed by a car – and Willie got her cat after all . . . Willie decided she didn't want her parents to go to Europe without her. Suddenly her mother, a concert pianist, was struck down by agonizing pains in her hands . . . And so the nightmare had begun . . .

0 552 10146 X   65p

A SELECTED LIST OF HORROR STORIES PUBLISHED BY CORGI BOOKS

All these books are available at your bookshop or newsagent, or can be ordered direct from the publisher. Just tick the titles you want and fill in the form below.

CORGI BOOKS, Cash Sales Department, P.O. Box 11, Falmouth, Cornwall.

Please send cheque or postal order, no currency.
U.K. send 19p for first book plus 9p per copy for each additional book ordered to a maximum charge of 73p to cover the cost of postage and packing.
B.F.P.O. and Eire allow 19p for first book plus 9p per copy for the next 6 books thereafter 3p per book.
Overseas Customers: Please allow 20p for the first book and 10p per copy for each additional book.

NAME (Block letters)..

ADDRESS ....

(JUNE 77)..

While every effort is made to keep prices low, it is sometimes necessary to increase prices at short notice. Corgi Books reserve the right to show new retail prices on covers which may differ from those previously advertised in the text or elsewhere.